Selected Tales of the
Brothers Grimm

Selected, Translated, and with an Afterword by Peter Wortsman

archipelago books

Based on the 7th edition of *Kinder- und Hausmärchen* published by the Brothers Grimm in 1857.

Archipelago Books
232 3rd Street #A111
Brooklyn, NY 11215
www.archipelagobooks.org

Library of Congress Cataloging-in-Publication Data available upon request.

Cover art: Pascale Monnin, 20 x 24 inches mixed media

The publication of *Selected Tales of the Brothers Grimm* was made possible with support from Lannan Foundation, the National Endowment for the Arts, and the New York State Council on the Arts, a state agency.

Contents

Foreword by
the Brothers Grimm*

We take comfort in the fact that when a storm or some other mishap hurled by the heavens thrashes an entire crop to the ground, among the low-growing hedgerow, or the bushes lining the way, a small patch is invariably spared and a few ears of grain withstand the onslaught. When the sun once again shines down on them, they keep on growing, solitary and unnoticed – no sickle fells them for the silo. But in late summer when they rear up ripe and full, hungry hands come to seek them out, laying them, ear upon precious ear, meticulously binding them in bundles, and far more prized than any other sheathes, they are carried home; they provide nourishment all winter long and even give seeds for future planting.

This is how it seemed to us, when we saw that of all that blossomed in former times nothing survived – even the memory thereof was almost erased – nothing, that is, but a few folk songs, a handful of books, some legends, and these innocent household tales. Hobbling kitchen stools by oven and hearth, stone stoops, holidays still celebrated, meadows and woods in their very solitude, and above all the untroubled imagination are the hedgerows that provided refuge in the storm, preserving them and facilitating their transmission from one age to another.

*Foreword to the second edition of Kinder- und Hausmärchen (1819).

It was perhaps high time to collect these fairy tales, for those who ought to safeguard them are fewer and fewer in number. Indeed, those few who still retain the knowledge of them tend to know a good many tales, for though other people pass away around them, they don't pass away for the people – but the custom of storytelling itself is on the wane, just like the knowledge of all those secret nooks in homes and gardens passed on from grandparent to grandchild, yielding to the constant shifting of an empty sense of splendor, a custom as elusive as the smile that plays on our lips when we speak of these household tales, a custom that may seem lavish though it costs but little. In those few places where they can still be found, fairy tales are such that we wouldn't think of asking if they're good or bad, poetic or insipid – we know them and love them precisely because this is how we first heard them, and we take pleasure in them without hesitation. How great is the grip of living custom: This, too, does poetry have in common with all the immutable constants of life, that we remain favorably disposed to it even when pressed by other priorities. We may, moreover, readily observe that fairy tales only took hold in places inclined to a more vibrant receptivity to poetry or where imagination has not yet been extinguished by the contrarieties of life. Yet neither will we, for the same reason, extol these fairy tales nor defend them in the face of contrary views: Their mere existence is enough of a safeguard. That which in so many ways and time and again delighted, moved, and educated carries its own imperative and surely derives from the same source that dabs all life with dew, and even if it were only a single drop caught by a little leaf, it nonetheless shimmers in the early-morning light.

Which is why this modest poesy is infused with a purity that seemed so wondrous and enchanting to us as children – these tales have, as it were, the same pale-blue, immaculately glimmering eyes that stay the same size, while the body's other parts are still so delicate, weak, and ill-equipped to stand their ground. This is the reason why with the present collection we do not merely wish to serve the history of poetry and mythology; it was also our intent that this poesy that comes alive and thrives in the delight it gives likewise serve as a primer for the very young. We did not for said purpose seek the kind of purity attained by the skittish elimination of all too common conditions and situations that dare not be denied, nor do we share the commonly held delusion that whatever appears in a printed book also happens in real life. We sought the kind of purity to be found in the truth of a straightforwardly told tale without any infelicities hidden in the manner of its telling. In the process of compiling this new edition we took pains to weed out every turn of phrase not appropriate for children. Should readers nevertheless object that here and there parents may find elements that make them bristle, and which they may deem objectionable, so that they would rather not put the book in children's hands, in certain cases they may be right, and they can easily make their own selection – but as a whole such measures are surely unnecessary for those with a healthy state of mind. Nothing can plead our case better than nature itself that made these flowers and leaves grow in just such a color and shape; should they not be held to be appropriate, according to any one person's special standards, he cannot insist that they should therefore be cut or colored differently. Or to put it another way, rain and dew fall as a blessing for everything that grows in the ground; whosoever dares not plant his sprouts outside because they are too delicate and might be damaged, but would rather grow them in his room and sprinkle them with distilled water, would not therefore demand the elimination of rain and dew. But all that's natural can thrive and this is what we should strive for. As a matter of fact, we know of no other healthy and powerful book compiled by the people, notably the Bible, in which certain questionable elements abound, more so than in our book; yet judicious practice finds nothing bad in this but, rather, as the saying goes, takes heart in it. Children fearlessly point at the stars, while others, bound by superstition, believe it disturbs the angels.

We have been collecting these fairy tales for some thirteen years; the first volume, which appeared in 1812, contained mostly what we gathered little by little from the folklore of Hessen, in the regions bordering on the Main and Kinzig rivers, in the county of Hanau, where we come from. The second volume, completed in 1814, was compiled in record time, partly because the project itself had made friends who helped us in our work, wherever needed, in the thrust and spirit of our intent, partly because fortune favored our endeavor, and happenstance conceded results to dogged and diligent collectors. For those who keep their eyes and ears open, such folk wisdom is more common than one might suppose, and this is particularly true of local customs and particularities, popular sayings and jests. Those splendid Low German fairy tales are the fruits of fortuitous kindness and friendship; the confidential nature of the dialect very much favors a narrative integrity. There in those fabled old bastions of German freedom, legends and fairy tales were preserved as an almost routine leisure and holiday form of entertainment, and the country is still rich with inherited customs and songs. There where, in part because the written word has not yet disrupted or blunted time-honored ways with a surfeit of foreign influence, in part because such inherited lore keeps memory from slacking off, particularly among peoples whose literature is deemed insignificant, folk traditions still serve as an all the more powerful and undiluted surrogate. So Lower Saxony appears to have preserved a greater store of such lore than all other regions. What a more comprehensive and richer collection might have been compiled in Germany in the sixteenth century, back in Hans Sachs's and Fischart's day.

It was one of those fortuitous coincidences that we happened to meet a peasant woman in the village of Niederzwehren, near Kassel, who told us the

majority and the most beautiful of the fairy tales in the second volume. Frau
Viehmännin was still fit and not much more than fifty years old. Her facial
expression had something firm, wise, and pleasant about it, and her big eyes
shone clear and sharp. She kept all the old legends firmly lodged in memory,
and she herself said that such a gift was not granted to all and that some
people couldn't remember anything. Her manner of telling was thoughtful,
deliberate, and uncommonly lively, clearly taking pleasure in the telling; she
would first tell it freely off the top of her head, and then, if asked to do so,
she would repeat it again slowly, so that with some practice one could record
the words. Certain elements have thus been preserved verbatim and will be
recognizable in their fidelity. Whoever may be inclined to suspect the slight-
est falsification of the traditional account, or any laxity in her retention of
the tale, and therefore, the impossibility of long-term preservation, ought
to have heard for himself just how precisely she stuck to the telling and how
meticulous she was; she never changed a word when retelling any part, and
promptly interrupted herself, correcting any inadvertent slip of the tongue on
the spot. The attachment to tradition is much stronger among such people
who live their lives in the selfsame way day in and day out than it is to those
of us inclined to countenance change. It is precisely for this reason that such
painstakingly preserved narratives display a certain emphatic immediacy and
intrinsic proficiency in the telling, which other more polished literary creations
never achieve. The epic fundament of all folklore is like the manifold shades
of green dispersed throughout nature that satisfy and soften our perception
without ever trying our patience.

In addition to the fairy tales in the second volume, we also received from
other similar sources countless supplements to the first and also many better
versions of tales we had included. As a mountainous country far off the beaten
track and mostly devoted to agriculture, Hessen has the advantage of being

better able to preserve old customs and traditions. A certain innate seriousness, and a healthy, industrious, and plucky disposition, which we are obliged to recognize, in addition to the size and comely stature of the men of this land, the original seat of the Chatts,[*] have thus been preserved; this, in contrast to the dainty and diminutive stature to be found in other lands, notably in Saxony, must rather be deemed an advantage. To the overall picture of which we must add the effect of a harsher, albeit often splendidly lovely, landscape, as well as a certain severity and gruffness in way of life. The Hessians must definitely be counted among those peoples in our German fatherland who, over the course of time, held most strongly to their characteristics as they did to their lands.

We wanted, therefore, to add to this second edition the material we had collected since the appearance of the first. So the first volume has been almost completely reworked, the incomplete fleshed out, some tales simplified and streamlined in the telling, and there are not many texts that were not in some way improved. We once again proofed suspect passages, that is, elements of foreign origin or supplements to the original, which we then proceeded to eliminate. Furthermore, we added new tales, including some from Austria and German-speaking parts of Bohemia, so that the reader will find some texts with which he is altogether unfamiliar. So it became possible not only to include what we had reluctantly removed from the original but also to add new passages that rightfully fit here, and which, we hope, will enhance the scholarly value of the whole.

As to the manner in which we collected this material, we were first and foremost beholden to fidelity and truthfulness. We did not, that is, add our own two cents, nor did we embellish any circumstance or feature of the legend but rather transmitted its contents as we received it; the fact that the phrasing

*A Germanic tribe native to Hessen.

and style of individual tales is largely ours seems self-evident, but we tried to preserve every idiosyncrasy we found so as in this regard to likewise leave our collection all the diversity found in nature. Anyone involved in a similar task will, moreover, readily admit that this cannot be deemed a casual and carefree endeavor; quite the contrary, a painstaking attentiveness and tact is called for, a set of skills that can only be acquired in the process, to distinguish the simpler, clearer, and yet more quintessential from the bowdlerized version. Whenever we found different versions of more or less the same tale that seemed to complete each other, and there were no contradictions that had to be excised in combining them, we presented the narrative as one, but if there were considerable variations, whereby each had its own unique traits, we favored what we thought to be the best version. These variations seemed more noteworthy to us than the kind that merely involved a slight modification and some tinkering with the established archetype, since the latter may, rather, merely constitute various attempts to approach the inexhaustible paradigm. Repetitions of individual sentences, narrative elements, and preludes must be viewed as nothing other than epic refrains that keep reoccurring whenever the tone shifts.

We gladly retained a distinctive dialect. Had we been able to do so throughout, the telling of each tale would doubtless have benefited. This is an instance in which cultivation, stylistic finessing, and artfulness prove detrimental, and one immediately fathoms that a refined written language, as dexterous, lucid, and clever as it might otherwise be, renders the telling more tasteless and corrupts the spirit of the original. It is a shame that the Low Saxon dialect spoken around Kassel, as well as in the border regions of the old Saxon and Frankish district of Hessen, is an imprecise and sadly inseparable mixture of Lower Saxon and High German.

To our knowledge no such collection of fairy tales exists in Germany. Either a few tales deemed worthy of transmission were preserved by chance or else

they were merely viewed as raw material around which to build more sub-
stantial stories. We herewith declare ourselves opposed precisely to such adaptations. It is indeed doubtless true that a poetic development and evolution
underlies every living poetic inclination, an ongoing development without
which any transmitted tradition would be sterile and stiff; this is precisely the
justifiable reason why every region has its own unique characteristics and
every dialect speaks in its own special way. But there is still a big difference
between that half-unconscious poetic development from the wellspring of life,
much like the quiet growth of plants, and a deliberate distortion of tradition
clipped and glued together based on altogether arbitrary criteria; it is this that
we cannot countenance. The only guideline then would be the poet's own
prevailing stance, a measure contingent on his cultivation, whereas the natural
development of the folk spirit prevails over that of the particular and does not
permit the expression of private appetites. If we concede a scholarly value in
oral tradition, that is, if we acknowledge that such lore contains the traces of
prehistoric outlook and culture, then it goes without saying that this value
is almost always undermined by such adaptations. Poetry itself has nothing
to gain from it. Then where else does it truly live than at that place where it
meets the soul, where it cools and refreshes or warms and fortifies? But those
adaptations of such legends that strip them of their simplicity, their innocence,
and their pristine purity tear them out of the context in which they belong and
where they are forever prized. It may be, and this is the best-case scenario, that
we add to the telling a certain finesse, a spirit, and in particular a wit that pokes
fun at the foolishness of the moment, a gentle elaboration of sentiment of the
sort often found in our common culture fed by the poetry of all peoples. But
this complement is more a matter of appearance than purpose – it presumes
the single listening or reading of the tale to which we've grown accustomed
in our time and gears itself up to that end. Such wit grows stale, however, in

the repetition, whereas the enduring narrative nuggets forever retain a certain calm, quiet, and purity in their effect. The studied hand of such adaptations is much like that of the gifted unfortunate, who turned everything he touched, including food, into gold, and thus, in the very lap of luxury, can neither still our appetite nor quench our thirst. Notwithstanding the mythological imagery meant to be conjured up by the sheer force of the imagination and with all those weighty and ponderous words, how barren, empty, and shapeless is the result! Our criticism, by the way, is only directed at such so-called adaptations that seek to embellish fairy tales and make them appear more poetic, not at a free interpretation of such tales that situate them as poetic expressions of the moment; for who would want to limit the poetic impulse by walling it in?

We pass this book on to sympathetic hands, cognizant of the beneficent strength of the tales it contains, and sincerely wish that its mysteries may remain invisible to those who would begrudge such crumbs of poetry to the poor and the needy among us.

Kassel, July 3, 1819

Selected Tales of the
Brothers Grimm

THE GOLDEN KEY

*O*nce in wintertime, when everything was covered in a deep bed of snow, a poor boy had to go out on his sled to fetch wood. After he had finished gathering and loading the wood, feeling frozen to the bone, before heading home he wanted to build a fire and warm himself a bit. So he scraped away the snow and cleared a patch of earth, when lo and behold, he found a little golden key lying there. Well, he figured, where there's a key there must also be a lock to fit it in, so he dug in the ground and found a little iron box. *If only the key fits!* he thought to himself. There must surely be precious things in the box. He looked and looked but could not find a keyhole; finally he found one, but it was so small he could hardly see it. He tried to insert the key and fortunately it fit. Then he turned it one time around, and now we will have to wait until he manages to open the lock and lift the lid to discover what sort of wondrous things are in the box.

THE SINGING BONE

Once upon a time a great lamentation arose in a certain land because of a wild boar that tore up the fields of the farmers, killed their livestock, and ripped open people's bodies with its tusks. The king offered a great reward to anyone who could rid the land of this calamity, but the beast was so big and strong that nobody dared to approach the forest in which it dwelled. Finally the king let it be known that whosoever captured or killed the wild boar would have the hand of his only daughter in marriage.

Now in this land there lived two brothers, sons of a poor man, who came to the king and were willing to take on this hazardous task. The elder brother, who was crafty and shrewd, offered his help out of pride; the younger brother, who was innocent and simple, did so out of the goodness of his heart. The king said, "So that you are all the more certain to find the beast, you will enter the forest from opposite sides." The elder one entered from where the sun sets and the younger one from where it rises. And after the younger brother had been walking a short while, a little man came up to him, holding a black spear in his hand, and said, "This spear I give you because your heart is pure and good. With it you may confidently set upon the wild boar, and it will do you no harm." The boy thanked the little man, hoisted the spear onto his shoulder, and continued fearlessly on his way. It wasn't long before he spotted the beast as it came charging at him. He held out the spear, and in the creature's rage it clove its heart in two. Then he lifted the monster onto his shoulder and carried it homeward, wanting to bring it to the king.

When he emerged at the forest's far side, he came upon an inn where people went to make merry with dance and wine. His elder brother had gone in, having thought to himself that the boar could wait and that before setting out he would first fortify himself with a glass or two. When he spotted his younger brother emerging from the forest with the prized carcass on his back, his envious and vindictive heart would not let him be. He called to him, "Do come in, dear brother, rest your weary bones and have a glass to refresh yourself." The younger brother, who suspected no evil intent, went in and told his brother of the kind little man who gave him the spear with which he killed the boar. The elder brother wined and dined him until evening, then the two set out together. But when in the dark of night they came to a bridge over a brook, the elder brother let the younger one go ahead, and halfway across the water struck him from behind so that he tumbled down dead. He buried him beneath the bridge, then took the boar and brought it to the king, pretending that it was he who killed it, whereupon, as promised, he received the king's daughter's hand in marriage. And when the younger brother failed to return, he said, "The boar must have mauled him," and everyone believed him.

But since nothing can remain hidden from the eyes of God, this dark deed, too, had to be revealed. Many years later a shepherd drove his herd across the bridge and spotted a snow-white bone lying below in the sand. He thought to himself, That would make a good mouthpiece. So he climbed down, picked it up, and carved himself a mouthpiece for his horn. But when he blew on it for the first time, to the shepherd's great surprise, the little bone started singing on its own:

"Oh, dear little shepherd boy,
The bone you blow on knows no joy,
My brother slayed me.
Beneath the bride he laid me
All for the wild boar's hide
To make the king's daughter his bride."

"What a wondrous little horn is this," said the shepherd, "an instrument that sings by itself. I must bring it to the king." And when he brought it before the king, the little horn started singing its song again. The king immediately understood its meaning, had the ground dug up under the bridge, and all the slaughtered brother's bones were unearthed. The evil brother could not deny the deed, was sewn up in a bag, and drowned, but the bones of the murdered one were laid to rest in the churchyard in a lovely grave.

THE TALE OF
THE JUNIPER TREE

I*t happened long, long ago*, more than two thousand years gone by. There was a rich man who had a beautiful and God-fearing wife, and they loved each other very much. But they had no children, much as they badly wanted them. And the woman prayed so hard day and night, but still she had no children, not a one.

Now in the yard, in front of their house, stood a juniper tree. One day in winter the woman stood beneath it, peeling herself an apple, and as she peeled she cut her finger, and the blood dripped into the snow. "Oh," said the woman with a deep sigh when she saw the blood in the snow, and suddenly felt overwhelmed with sadness, "if only I had a child as red as blood and as white as snow." Having let these words spill from her lips, she felt a great happiness, and she was certain it would come to pass.

So she went back into the house, and after a month went by the snow melted. After two months, everything was green. After three months, flowers blossomed from the ground. After four months, all the trees in the forest grew heavy with leaves, and the green branches were all entwined with one another. And the little birds twittered so that the entire forest resounded with their song, and the blossoms fell from the trees. Then a fifth month had gone by, and she stood again beneath the juniper tree; it smelled so sweet her heart nearly burst for joy, and she fell to her knees and was beside herself with emotion. And after the sixth month had lapsed, the fruit hung thick and plump, and she fell still. At the end of the seventh month, she picked all the juniper berries and gobbled them down so greedily it made her sick and solemn. The eighth month passed, and she called her husband to her. Weeping, she said to him, "If I die, bury me under the juniper tree." Then she felt greatly relieved and happy, and at the end of the ninth month she bore a child as white as snow and as red as blood, and when she set eyes on the child she was so glad that she died.

Her husband buried her beneath the juniper tree, and he cried and cried inconsolably. In time he felt a little better, and although he still shed tears at least his grief was bearable. And not long after that he took another wife.

With the second wife he had a daughter, but the child he'd had with his first wife was a little son, and he was as red as blood and as white as snow. When the woman looked at her daughter she loved her a lot, but then she looked at the little lad and it gnawed at her heart to see him, as if he would forever stand in the way, and she couldn't stop thinking how to keep the inheritance all for her daughter. And the Evil One wouldn't let up, so that she was altogether filled with hatred for the little lad. She kept shoving him around from one place to another, and slapped him here and whacked him there, so that the poor little fellow was frightened all the time. As soon as he came home from school he could find no place of refuge from her wrath.

Once when the woman went up to her room, her little daughter came bounding up the stairs after her and said, "Mother, give me an apple."

"Yes, my child," said the woman, and took a luscious-looking apple from the chest and gave it to her. The chest had a great big heavy lid with a large sharp iron lock.

"Mother," said the little girl, "will my brother not get one too?"

The woman winced, but she said, "Yes, when he comes home from school." And when, peering out the window, she saw him coming, it was as if the Evil One grabbed hold of her, and she reached out and took back the apple from her daughter and said, "You shan't have one before your brother." Then she flung the apple back into the chest and locked it. Whereupon the little lad walked through the door, and the Evil One made her speak sweetly to him. "My son," she said, "would you like to have an apple?" And she gave him such a nasty look.

"Mother," said the little fellow, "how cross you look! Yes, give me an apple."

She felt as if she had to convince him. "Come with me," she said, lifting the lid, "and pick out an apple." And when the little boy bent over, the Evil One beckoned, and blam! She slammed the lid so that his head was chopped off and landed among the red apples. Riddled with fear at what she'd done, she thought to herself, I've got to find a way to get out of this! Then she went up to her room, opened her chest of drawers, and pulled a white scarf out of the top drawer, set the boy's head back on his neck, wrapped the scarf around it so that nobody could see that it was severed, propped him up on a stool in front of the door, and put the apple in his hand.

Not long after that Marlenikin came over to her mother in the kitchen, who was standing by the fire, stirring and stirring a pot of hot water. "Mother," said Marlenikin, "my brother is seated by the door all white in the face with an apple in his hand. I asked him to give me the apple but he made no reply. The sight of him gives me the creeps."

"Go back to him," said the mother, "and if he still says nothing, give him a cuff on the ear."

So Marlenikin went and said, "Brother, give me the apple." But when he made no reply, she boxed his ear, whereupon his head fell off. Then she panicked and started crying and screaming. And she ran to her mother and said, "Oh, Mother, I knocked my brother's head off," and kept crying and crying and would not stop crying.

"Marlenikin," said the mother, "what have you done! Better be quiet now, if you don't want anyone to know. No point crying over spilt milk. We'll boil him up and make a stew." Then the mother took the little boy and hacked him into pieces, put the pieces in the pot, and prepared a stew. But Marlenikin stood beside her and kept crying and crying, and her tears fell in the pot, so it needed no salt.

Then the father came home, sat himself down at the table, and said, "Where is my son?"

The mother served him up a great big helping of stew, and Marlenikin wouldn't stop crying.

The father asked again, "Where is my son?"

"Oh," said the woman, "he took a trip to visit his mother's great-uncle. He'll stay there for a while."

"What in heaven's name is he doing there? He didn't even say goodbye to me?"

"Oh, well, he wanted to go so badly, and asked if he could stay six weeks. I'm sure they'll take good care of him there."

The man replied, "I'm so sad, it isn't right that he should have left without saying goodbye." Whereupon he started eating, and said, "Marlenikin, why are you crying? Your brother will be back soon." Then he said, "Woman, this stew tastes so good, give me more!" And the more he ate, the more he wanted, and he said, "Give me more, the two of you shall have none. It seems to me as if it were all mine." And he ate and ate, and dropped all the bones under the table, until he had gobbled it all up.

Then Marlenikin went to her chest of drawers, drew her best silken scarf from the bottom drawer, and gathered all the bones little and big from under the table, bound them in her silken scarf, and hauled them out the door, where she wept bloody tears. She laid the bones out in the green grass under the juniper tree, and once she had done so she felt a whole lot better and didn't cry anymore.

After that the juniper tree started to sway, and the branches spread farther and farther apart and then came back together again, as if in a burst of joy someone were clapping his hands. And it was as if a mist rose from the tree, and in the midst of the mist a fire burned, and a beautiful bird flew out of the fire. It sang so sweetly and flew high up in the air, and once it was gone the juniper tree was again as before, and the cloth with the bones was gone. But Marlenikin felt so giddy and glad-hearted, as if her brother were still alive. Then she went cheerfully back into the house, sat down at the table, and ate.

But the bird flew away, landed on the roof of a goldsmith's house, and started singing:
"My mother, she smote me,
My father, he ate me,
My sister, sweet Marlenikin,
Gathered all my little bonikins,
Bound them in a silken scarf,
And lay them under the juniper tree.
Tweet, tweet, I'm a pretty birdie, look at me!"
The goldsmith, who sat at his workbench fashioning a golden chain, heard the bird perched on his rooftop singing. The song sounded so sweet to him that he got up to have a look, and as he crossed his doorstep he lost a slipper.

But he strode out into the middle of the street with only one slipper and one sock on, draped in his leather apron and with the golden chain in one hand and his tongs in the other. And the sun shone brightly on that street. He stepped forward, then stood still and said to the bird, "Your song is so sweet, will you sing it again?"

"No," said the bird, "I won't sing it a second time for nothing. Give me the golden chain and I'll do as you ask."

"Here," said the goldsmith, "take the golden chain, and sing it again."

Then the bird swooped down and snatched the golden chain with its right claw, landed in front of the goldsmith, and sang:

"My mother, she smote me,

My father, he ate me,

My sister, sweet Marlenikin,

Gathered all my little bonikins,

Bound them in a silken scarf,

And lay them under the juniper tree.

Tweet, tweet, I'm a pretty birdie, look at me!"

Then the bird flew to a shoemaker, landed on his rooftop, and sang:

"My mother, she smote me,

My father, he ate me,

My sister, sweet Marlenikin,

Gathered all my little bonikins,

Bound them in a silken scarf,

And lay them under the juniper tree.

Tweet, tweet, I'm a pretty birdie, look at me!"

Entranced by the song, the shoemaker ran out the door in his shirtsleeves, peered up at his roof, and held his hand in front of his eyes to keep from being blinded by the sun. "Bird," said he, "you sure can sing." Then he called to his wife through the open door: "Honey, why don't you come out and get a load of this bird here, boy can it ever sing!" Then he called to his daughter and her children, to the journeymen, the apprentice, and the maid, and they all came out into the street to have a look at the bird; they saw how beautiful it was with its red-and-green plumage, and around its neck it wore a golden chain, and its eyes twinkled like stars. "Bird," said the shoemaker, "sing me that ditty again."

"No," said the bird, "I won't sing it a second time for nothing, you've got to give me something."

"Honey," said the man to his wife, "go to the shop and bring me the pair of red shoes on the top shelf." So his wife went and fetched the shoes. "Here, bird," said the man, "now sing me that ditty one more time."

Then the bird swooped down, grabbed hold of the shoes with its left claw, and flew back up to the rooftop and sang:

"My mother, she smote me,
My father, he ate me,
My sister, sweet Marlenikin,
Gathered all my little bonikins,
Bound them in a silken scarf,
And lay them under the juniper tree.
Tweet, tweet, I'm a pretty birdie, look at me!"

And once it had sung the song to the end, it flew away. With the golden chain in its right claw and the shoes in its left, it flew to a mill. And the mill went: "Clip-clop, clip-clop, clip-clop." And in the mill sat twenty apprentices hammering and chiseling away at a millstone: "Slam-bam, slam-bam, slam-bam." And the mill went: "Clip-clop, clip-clop, clip-clop." The bird landed on a juniper tree that stood in front of the mill and sang:

"My mother, she smote me."

Whereupon one apprentice stopped what he was doing.

"My father, he ate me."

Two more stopped working and listened up.

"My sister, sweet Marlenikin."

Four more stopped to listen.

"Gathered all my little bonikins,
Bound them in a silken scarf."

Now only eight kept hammering.

"And lay them under . . ."

Now only five.

". . . The juniper tree."

Now just one.

"Tweet, tweet, I'm a pretty birdie, look at me!"

Then the last one also stopped what he was doing and heard the last words of the song. "Bird," said he, "you sing so sweetly! I'd like to hear it all, sing it to me one more time."

"No," said the bird, "I won't sing it a second time for nothing. If you give me the millstone I'll sing it again."

"If it belonged to me alone," he said, "you could have it."

"Okay," the others agreed, "if the bird sings it again he can have it."

Then the bird came flying down, and twenty millers heaved a beam and lifted up the stone, with an "Ally-oop, ally-oop, ally-oop!"

Whereupon the bird poked its head through the hole in the millstone, and wearing it like a collar, flew back up to the tree and sang:

"My mother, she smote me,
My father, he ate me,
My sister, sweet Marlenikin,
Gathered all my little bonikins,
Bound them in a silken scarf,

And lay them under the juniper tree.

Tweet, tweet, I'm a pretty birdie, look at me!"

And having sung it to the end, the bird flapped its wings, with the chain in its right claw, the shoes in its left, and the millstone around its neck, and flew off to the father's house.

There at the table sat the father, the mother, and Marlenikin, and the father said, "I feel so glad-hearted, so happy through and through."

"Not me," said the mother. "I feel a deep dread, as if a dark storm were headed our way."

But Marlenikin just sat there, crying her eyes out.

Then the bird came flying up and landed on the rooftop, and the father said, "I feel as good as gold, and the sun is shining so brightly outside. I've got a funny feeling I'm going to meet again someone near and dear to me."

"Not me," said the wife. "I'm so scared my teeth are rattling and my blood runs like fire through my veins." And she tore open her bodice to breathe a little better.

But Marlenikin sat crying in a corner, and holding a handkerchief to her eyes she soaked it through and through with her tears.

Then the bird landed on the juniper tree and sang:

"My mother, she smote me."

Whereupon the mother held her ears and eyes shut so as not to hear or see, but there was a terrible tempest storming in her ears and her eyes burned like they were struck with lightning.

"My father, he ate me."

"Oh, Mother," said the man, "there's a pretty bird singing so sweetly, and the sun-baked air's so warm. I swear it smells like cinnamon."

"My sister, sweet Marlenikin," sang the bird.

Whereupon the girl lay her head on her knees and wept like there was no tomorrow.

But the man said, "I've got to go out and see that bird up close."

"Don't go, I beg you," said the woman. "It feels like the whole house were on fire, every timber trembling."

But the man went out and peered at the bird.

"Gathered all my little bonikins,
Bound them in a silken scarf,
And lay them under the juniper tree.
Tweet, tweet, I'm a pretty birdie, look at me!"

Whereupon the bird dropped the golden chain and it fell around the man's neck, and it landed so lithely that it fit him just right. Then he went back inside and said, "Will you look at that, the pretty bird gave me a lovely golden chain, and it looks terrific on me."

But the woman was so frightened she fell down flat on the floor and her cap tumbled off her head.

Then the bird sang it again:

"My mother, she smote me."

"If only I were a thousand fathoms underground, so I wouldn't have to hear that infernal twitter!"

"My father, he ate me."

The woman collapsed like she was dead.

"My sister, sweet Marlenikin."

"Oh," said Marlenikin, "I too want to go out to see if the bird will give me something." So she went out.

"Gathered all my little bonikins,
Bound them in a silken scarf."

Then the bird tossed her the shoes.

"And lay them under the juniper tree.

Tweet, tweet, I'm a pretty birdie, look at me!"

Now she was happy as could be. She donned the new red shoes, dancing and jumping for joy. "Oh," she said, "I was so sad when I went out and now I'm giddy with glee. That wonderful bird just gave me a pair of red shoes."

"No," cried the woman and leapt up with her hair standing on end, like it was on fire. "I feel like the world was about to go under, let me go out too and see if it makes me feel any better."

And as she stepped out the door, blam! The bird dropped the millstone on her head so that she was crushed flat as a pancake. The father and Marlenikin heard the crash and went out to see what happened. A great column of smoke and shooting flames rose from the spot, and when the fire had burned itself out there stood the little brother, and he took his father and Marlenikin by the hand, and the three of them were so very happy, they went inside and sat down to eat.

HANSEL AND GRETEL

O*n the edge* of a deep, dark forest there lived a poor woodcutter with his wife and his two children; the boy's name was Hansel and the girl was named Gretel. The woodcutter had little to nibble or gnaw on, and once, when there was great famine in the land, he could no longer even bring home his daily crust of bread. As he kept ruminating and tossing and turning that evening in bed, he let out a sigh and said to his wife, "What will become of us? How can we feed our poor children, as we ourselves have nothing to eat?"

"You know what, husband," replied his wife, "tomorrow bright and early we'll take the children into the woods to where it's darkest and deepest. There we'll light them a fire and leave them a last few crumbs of bread, then we'll go about our business and leave them there. They'll never find their way home again and we'll be rid of them."

"No, woman," said the man, "I will not do that. How can I ever find it in my heart to leave my children in the woods alone? The wild animals would soon come and tear them to pieces."

"Oh, you fool," she said, "then all four of us will starve to death. All you'll

have left to do is plane the planks for our coffins." And she would not let up until he agreed.

"Still I feel sorry for my poor children all the same," said the man.

But hunger kept the two children awake and they overheard what their stepmother said to their father. Gretel cried bitter tears and said to Hansel, "Now we're done for."

"Quiet, Gretel," said Hansel. "Don't worry, I'll find a way out." And once the grown-ups had fallen asleep, he got up, put on his little coat, opened the back door, and slipped out. The moon shone very brightly, and the white pebbles scattered in front of the house glistened like silver. Hansel bent down and stuffed his coat pockets to bursting. Then he went back in and said to Gretel, "Calm yourself, my dear little sister, and sleep tight, God will not forsake us," and he lay back down in his bed.

At the break of day, even before sunrise, the woman came and woke the two children. "Get up, you lazybones, we're going to the forest to fetch wood." Then she gave each of them a crust of bread and said, "Here's something for the midday meal, but don't eat it before then, for you'll get nothing else." Gretel took the bread into her apron pocket, because Hansel already had his pockets full of pebbles, then they all set off for the forest. After they had walked for a while, Hansel stopped and peered back at the house, and did it again and again.

The father said, "Hansel, why do you keep looking back and lagging behind? Watch where you're going and shake a leg."

"Oh, Father," said Hansel, "I'm looking back at my little white cat that's seated on the rooftop and wants to say goodbye."

The woman said, "Fool, that's no cat, that's the rising sun shining on the chimney." But Hansel hadn't been looking at his cat, for each time he turned he dropped a white pebble from his pocket on the path.

Once they'd reached the heart of the forest, the father said, "Go fetch wood, children, I'll build you a fire so that you don't freeze." Hansel and Gretel gathered brushwood, a whole heap of it.

The brushwood was lighted, and when the flames burned high, the woman said, "Now lay yourselves down beside the fire, children, and rest up. We're going into the forest to cut wood. When we're done, we'll come back and get you."

Hansel and Gretel sat by the fire, and when midday came, each ate their little crust of bread. And because they heard the sound of the wood ax chopping, they thought their father was near. But it was not the ax, it was a branch their father had tied to a withered tree, which the wind rattled back and forth. And as they had sat there waiting a long while, their eyes grew heavy with fatigue and they fell fast asleep. When at last they woke up it was already the dead of night. Gretel started crying. "How will we ever find our way out of the woods!"

But Hansel comforted her. "Just wait for a while until the moon rises, and we'll find our way all right." And when the full moon had risen, Hansel took his little sister by the hand and followed the white pebbles; they shimmered like newly minted coins and showed him the way. They walked the whole night and at daybreak got back to their father's house.

They knocked at the door, and the woman opened it, saw that it was Hansel and Gretel, and said, "You naughty children, why did you sleep so long in the woods? We thought you'd never come home." But the father, whose heart was heavy at having left them behind in the woods, was overjoyed to see his children again.

Not long thereafter, things got bad again all over the land, and the children overheard their stepmother say to their father in bed at night, "We're scraping the barrel again, all we have left is half a loaf of bread, and then we're done for. The children have to go. We'll take them deeper into the forest this time so that they won't find their way back, or else we're goners." The man felt bad, and thought, Better I should share my last bite with my children. But the woman wouldn't listen to anything he said and kept on complaining and badgering him. One mistake leads to another, and because he had given in the first time he had to give in again.

But the children were still awake and had overheard the conversation. As soon as the grown-ups were asleep, Hansel got up again and wanted to go out to gather pebbles as he had the last time, but the woman had locked the door and Hansel could not get out. Still he comforted his little sister and said, "Don't cry, Gretel, and sleep tight. God will help us, you'll see."

Early the next morning the woman came to drag the children out of bed. They each received a crust of bread that was even smaller than the last time. On the way into the woods, Hansel crumbled it in his pocket, often stopping to toss a crumb on the ground. "Hansel, why are you just standing there looking around," said the father. "Shake a leg."

"I'm looking after my little pigeon that's perched on the rooftop and wants to wave goodbye," replied Hansel.

"Fool," said the woman, "that's no pigeon, that's the morning sun shining on the chimney." But Hansel kept on dropping bread crumbs along the way.

The woman led the children deeper and deeper into the woods, where they'd never been before. Another big fire was lit, and the stepmother said, "Just sit here, children, and when you get tired you can take a little nap. We're going into the forest to cut wood, and in the evening when we're done, we'll come and get you."

At midday, Gretel shared her bread with Hansel, who had crumbled and scattered his share along the way. Then they nodded off to sleep and darkness fell, but nobody came to pick up the poor children. They awakened in the dead of night and Hansel comforted his little sister and said, "Just wait, Gretel, until the moon rises, then we'll see the bread crumbs I scattered and they'll show us the way home." When the moon rose they set out, but they could not find any bread crumbs, for the flocks of birds that circle woods and fields had eaten them up. They walked all night and another day from morning until evening, but they never made it out of the woods and were very hungry, as they'd eaten nothing but a few berries they found on the ground. And because they were so tired, and their little legs couldn't carry them any farther, they lay themselves down under a tree and fell asleep.

It was already the third morning since they'd left their father's house. They began walking again, but they went ever deeper into the woods, and if help did not reach them soon they were done for. At noon they spotted a lovely little snow-white bird perched on a branch, which sang so sweetly they stopped and listened. And when it was done singing, it flapped its wings and fluttered before them, and they followed it until they came to a little cottage on the roof of which the bird landed, and when the children approached they saw that the cottage was built out of bread and covered with cake, but the windows were made of clear sugar crystal.

"Let's dig in," said Hansel, "and make a blessed meal of it. I'll eat a piece of the roof, and you, Gretel, can sup on the window, which ought to taste sweet." Hansel reached out and broke off a little bit of the roof to see how it tasted, and Gretel walked up to the windowpane and nibbled at it. Whereupon a soft voice called out from within:

"Nibble, nibble, like a mouse,

Who is nibbling at my house?"

To which the children replied:

"The wind blows wild,

The heavenly child,"

and kept right on eating without batting a lash.

Hansel, to whom the roof tasted delicious, tore off a great big hunk of it, and Gretel pried off a whole round windowpane, sat herself down, and promptly ate it up. Then all of a sudden the door flew open and an old crone came hobbling out on a crutch. Hansel and Gretel were so petrified they dropped what they had in their hands. But the old woman just shook her head and said, "Oh my dear little children, who brought you here? Come in, come in, and make yourselves at home, no harm will come to you here." Then she took both of them by the hand and led them into her little house. She fetched all kinds of good things to eat, milk and pancakes with sugar, apples and nuts. And afterward, she made up two little beds with fresh white linen, and Hansel and Gretel lay themselves down and thought they were in heaven.

But the old woman only pretended to be nice. She was an evil witch who lay in wait for children and had only built the house of bread to lure them into a trap. Whenever she got her hands on a fresh young thing, she cooked it up and made a feast of it. Witches have red eyes and can't see very far, but they have a keen sense of smell, like animals, and know when people are approaching. When Hansel and Gretel came up close to her house, she snickered and sneered to herself, "I've got them in the bag, they won't get away."

Early the next morning, before the children batted a lash and still lay lost in their sweet slumber, she got up to peer at their round, rosy cheeks, and muttered to herself, "They'll make a tasty morsel." Whereupon she grabbed Hansel with her bony-fingered hand, dragged him out to a little pen, and locked him behind a wire gate. Cry as he might, it did him no good. Then she went over to Gretel, shook her awake, and yelled, "Get up, you lazybones, fetch me water from the well and cook your brother something good to eat. He's out there in the pen and I mean to fatten him up. And when he's good and plump, I'll eat him." Gretel started crying bitterly, but it did her no good, she had to do what the evil witch wanted.

So the finest food was cooked up for poor Hansel, yet Gretel got nothing but crayfish shells. Every morning the old crone slipped off to the pen and cried, "Hansel, stick your finger out so I can feel if you're fat enough." But Hansel poked a little bone out of the pen, and the old crone, whose eyes were weak and couldn't see it, took it for Hansel's finger, surprised that he had failed to fatten up. Once four weeks had gone by and Hansel still stayed skinny, she was gripped by impatience and couldn't wait any longer. "Get a move on, Gretel!" she cried to the girl. "Be quick and fetch me water – Hansel may be fat or lean, but tomorrow I'll slaughter and cook him."

Oh how the poor little sister wailed as she carried the water, and oh what a flood of tears ran down her cheeks! "God help us!" she cried out. "If only the wild animals in the woods had eaten us, as least we would have died together."

"Save your whimpering," said the old crone, "it won't do you any good."

Early the next morning Gretel had to go out to light a fire and put the kettle to boil. "First we'll bake," said the hag. "I already lit the oven and kneaded the dough." She prodded the poor girl over to the oven, from which flames shot out. "Crawl in," said the witch, "and see if it's hot enough to bake the bread." Once Gretel had poked her head in the witch intended to slam the oven door shut, to roast her and eat her.

But Gretel grasped what she had in mind, and said, "I don't know how to do it. How am I supposed to climb in?"

"Foolish ninny," said the old crone, "as you can see for yourself, the opening is even big enough for me to climb in," whereupon she came hobbling over and poked her head in. Then Gretel gave her a shove so that she went tumbling in, heaved the iron door shut, and slipped the latch. Then the witch started howling something awful – "Ayyyyy!" And Gretel ran off, and the godless witch was burned to a crisp.

But Gretel scampered straight to Hansel, opened the pen, and cried out, "Hansel, we're saved, the old witch is dead." And as soon as the gate was opened, Hansel came flying out like a bird from a cage. How they rejoiced, fell into each other's arms, leapt for joy, and covered each other with kisses! And because they had nothing more to fear, they went back into the witch's house, in every corner of which stood cupboards filled with pearls and precious stones.

"They're better than pebbles," said Hansel, and stuffed as many as he could fit in his pockets.

And Gretel said, "I think I'll take some too," and filled her apron with them.

"We'd better go now and get out of the witch's woods," said Hansel. But after they'd walked for hours, they came to a great big lake. "We can't get across," said Hansel. "I don't see a ford or footbridge."

"There's no boat either," said Gretel, "but there's a little white duck swimming along. If I ask it, maybe it will help us get across." And she called out:

"Duckling, duckling, soft and white,

There's no ford or footbridge in sight.

Gretel and Hansel beg you with a quack:

Carry us across on your soft white back."

The duckling came swimming up, and Hansel sat himself on its back and bid his sister sit beside him. "No," replied Gretel, "the little duck can't bear the weight of us both. Let it ferry us across one after the other." The kind little creature did just that, and once they were safely across, the woods looked more and more familiar, and finally they glimpsed from afar their father's house. Then they started running, burst in, and fell into their father's arms. The man had not had a moment of peace ever since he left his children in the woods, but the woman had died. Gretel shook her apron out, so that the pearls and precious stones spilled all over the room, and Hansel emptied his pockets, one fistful after another. Their troubles had come to an end, and they lived happily together.

My fairy tale too has come to an end. There's a mouse running there, and whoever catches it can make himself a big fur hat.

THE GOLDEN GOOSE

There once was a man who had three sons, the youngest of whom was called "Simpleton" and was scorned and ridiculed and slighted time and again. It so happened one day that the eldest son had to go to the forest to cut wood, and before he left, his mother gave him a lovely-looking and delicious pancake and a bottle of wine to satisfy his hunger and quench his thirst. At the forest's edge he happened upon a little gray man who bid him good day and said, "Give me a piece of the pancake in your pocket and let me have a swallow of your wine. I'm so hungry and thirsty."

To which the savvy son replied, "If I give you my pancake and my wine I'll have none left for myself. Be off with you!" So he left the stranger high and dry and continued on his way. But when he started cutting down a tree it wasn't long before he took a bad swing and the ax struck him in the arm, so that he had to return home and get himself bandaged up. This happened on account of his treatment of the little gray man.

Then the second son went to the forest, and just as she had done with the

eldest, the mother gave him a pancake and a bottle of wine. He too encountered the little gray man, who stopped him to ask for a bite of his pancake and a swallow of his wine. But the second son sensibly replied, as had the first, "Whatever I give you will be all the less for me. Be off with you!" And he left the little man high and dry and continued on his way. The punishment followed promptly; with a misguided swing of the ax at a tree he struck himself in the leg and had to be carried back home.

Then Simpleton said, "Father, let me go cut wood."

To which the father replied, "Your brothers landed themselves some nasty gashes in the process, better not try. You don't know how to cut wood." But Simpleton pleaded so long that the father finally said, "Go then if you must. The wounds may make you wise."

The mother gave him a water-based cake baked in ashes and a bottle of sour beer. When he got to the forest he also met the little old gray man, who greeted him and said, "Give me a piece of your cake and a swig from your bottle. I'm so hungry and thirsty."

To which Simpleton replied, "I only have ash cake and sour beer, but if that's good enough for you, let's sit down and eat."

Then they sat down and Simpleton pulled out his ash cake, but it was a splendid pancake, and his sour beer had turned into fine wine. So they ate and drank, and after that the little man said, "Because you have a good heart and shared what's yours, I will grant you good fortune. Yonder stands an old tree. Cut it down, and you will find something at its roots." Whereupon the stranger took his leave.

Simpleton went over and hacked down the tree, and as it fell, there at the roots sat a goose with feathers of pure gold. He picked it up, took it with him, and went to an inn to spend the night. But the innkeeper had three daughters who saw the goose, were curious what kind of wondrous bird it was, and craved one of its golden feathers. The eldest thought, I'll find an occasion to pluck out a feather. And when Simpleton happened to go out she grabbed the goose by one of its wings, but her hand got stuck. Not long after that the second sister was dead set on the same, to pluck out a feather – but no sooner did she touch her sister than she got stuck. Finally the third sister came with the same idea, but the others screamed, "Stay back, for heaven's sake, stay back." But she did not fathom why she should stay away, and thought, If they're at it, I might as well join in. And so she leapt forward, and as soon as she touched the middle sister's hand, she too got stuck. So they had to spend the night with the goose.

The following morning Simpleton took the goose under his arm and went on his way, not concerning himself with the three girls stuck to it. They had to keep running after him, left right, left right, according to the rhythm of his step. In the middle of a field they met a pastor, and when he saw the entourage he said, "You ought to be ashamed of yourselves, you nasty girls, to be running after that young boy through hill and dale. It's just not right." At these words, he grabbed the youngest by the hand to tear her away – but as soon as he touched her, he too got stuck and had to run along behind them.

Not long after that the sexton came and saw the pastor following the three girls. Very much surprised, he called out, "Hey, pastor, what's the hurry? Don't forget that we still have a baptism to officiate today." He ran after him and grabbed him by the sleeve, and promptly got stuck. Two peasants came strolling out of the field dragging a hoe, surprised to see the five of them trudging along. The pastor pleaded for them to release the sexton and himself. But as soon as they touched the sexton's hand, they too got stuck, and now there were seven running after Simpleton and his golden goose.

They soon came to a city ruled by a king who had a daughter so somber and serious nobody could make her laugh. Therefore he passed a law that whosoever could make her laugh would have her as his bride. When Simpleton heard this, he went with his goose and his entourage to present himself to the princess, and as soon as she saw the seven souls running after him she split her sides laughing and couldn't stop. So Simpleton asked for her hand in marriage, but the king, hardly inclined to accept such a son-in-law, raised all sorts of objections and said that he first had to bring him a man who could drink up a cellar-full of wine.

Simpleton, thinking that the little gray man might be able to help, went out into the forest, and at the spot where he had cut down the tree he saw a man seated there with a sad expression on his face. Simpleton asked what caused him such a heavy heart, to which the man replied, "I have such a mighty thirst I can't quench it. I can't abide cold water. I've already guzzled down a cask of wine, but that's just a drop in the bucket."

"I can help you," said Simpleton. "Come with me, and you'll drink your fill." He took him to the king's wine cellar, and the man promptly attacked the casks. He drank until his sides ached, and before the day was done he had drunk up the entire cellar.

Simpleton once again demanded his bride, but the king could not abide that such a lowly fellow whom everyone called Simpleton should carry off his daughter, and so set new stipulations. He first had to find a man who could eat up a mountain of bread. Simpleton didn't hesitate for long but went straight to the woods, and there at the same spot sat a man with a strap tied tightly around his middle and a dour look, who said, "I gobbled up an entire oven-full of bread crumbs, but it's no use, I'm still so hungry. My belly's empty and I have to tighten my belt, lest I die of hunger."

Simpleton smiled and said, "Get up and come with me, and you'll eat your fill." He led him to the king's court, where the king had amassed all the flour in his realm, which he'd had baked into a prodigious mountain of bread. But the man from the forest set to it and started eating, and in a day's time the entire mountain of bread was gone.

So for a third time Simpleton demanded his bride, but the king sought yet another pretext to refuse, demanding a ship that could sail on land and water. "As soon as you come sailing up in such a vessel," he said, "I'll give you my daughter's hand in marriage."

So Simpleton went straight back to the forest. Seated at the selfsame spot he found the little gray man, who said, "For you I drank and ate, and I'll get you the vessel too – all because you were merciful to me." Then he gave him the ship that could sail on land and water, and as soon as the king saw Simpleton sailing up to the castle he could no longer refuse him his daughter. The wedding was celebrated, and after the king's death Simpleton inherited the kingdom and lived a long life with his wife.

THE OWL

Several centuries ago, when people weren't half as canny and shrewd as they are today, a curious occurrence came to pass in a small town. One of those great big owls called Shuhus flew into town from the neighboring woods one night, took refuge in the barn of a respected burgher, and fearing the other birds, who, upon seeing it, gave off an awful squall, didn't dare come out again. When the farmhand entered the barn the following morning to gather hay, he took such a terrible fright at the sight of the owl seated in the corner that he ran away and reported to his master that a monster the likes of which he had never seen was seated in the barn, its great eyes rotating in its head, liable to gobble you up in a single bite.

"I know your kind," said the master. "You're brave enough to hunt down a blackbird in the field, but spot a dead chicken and you'll first find a stick to poke it before drawing near. Let me go see for myself what kind of monster it is," the master added, courageously entering the barn and looking around. But when he saw the strange and terrible creature with his own eyes, he took no less a fright than his farmhand. Howling a string of words to himself, he trundled out of the barn, ran to his neighbors, and begged them to stand by him to face the unknown and terrible creature, lest the entire town risk its wrath were it to break out of his barn where it sat.

A great hubbub arose in the streets. The burghers came armed with pikes, pitchforks, scythes, and axes, as though they meant to make war on the enemy. They were joined by all the councilmen, led by the mayor. Once they'd gathered in the marketplace, they set out for the barn and surrounded it on all sides, whereupon one of the bravest of the lot stepped forward and entered the barn with his sharpened pike raised. But he promptly came running back out again, pale as death and unable to utter a word. Two others dared enter, but they fared no better.

Finally a big strong man stepped forward, famous hereabouts for his feats of bravery in war, and said, "It won't do any good just to ogle the beast, we need a plan. But I can see that you've all gone yellow and not one of you dares bite the fox by its tail." He had them bring him a suit of armor, a sword, and a spear, and readied himself to do battle. Everyone marveled at his pluck but feared for his life. The two doors were flung open and all present caught site of the owl that had in the meantime perched on a big crossbeam in the middle of the barn. The brave man had a ladder brought in, and as he set it in place and prepared to climb, everyone told him to hold firm, as did Saint George when he tilted with the dragon. Once he'd climbed to the top and the owl saw the man draw near, befuddled by the mob below and the cry of the crowd, and not knowing how to get out, it rotated its eyes, ruffled its feathers, spread its wings, snapped its beak, and let out its stentorian *"Shuhu, Shuhu."*

"Heave to, heave to!" the crowd outside cried to the brave hero.

"Anyone standing where I'm standing," he replied, "wouldn't cry: Heave to!" He raised a foot to climb another rung, then started to tremble, and half faint with fear, posted a hasty retreat.

Now there was no one left to face the danger. "By just snapping and breathing upon him," they said, "the monster poisoned the strongest man among us, sending him to his grave. Should we too lay our lives on the line?" They put their heads together to try to figure out what to do to save the city.

For the longest time it seemed like there was no way out, until finally the mayor came up with a plan. "In my opinion," he said, "we pool our resources to buy this barn, including everything in it, grain, straw, and hay, from the owner, and then we burn it all to the ground, the terrible creature along with it, so that nobody need risk his life. There's no time to lose, we dare spare no expense." Everyone agreed. So the barn was set on fire from all four corners and the poor owl went down along with it. If you don't believe me, just go there and ask for yourself.

A FAIRY TALE ABOUT
A BOY WHO SET OUT
TO LEARN FEAR

A*father had two sons.* The elder one was savvy and smart and able to attend to every task at hand. But the younger one was a fool unable to grasp or learn anything. When people saw him, they said, "The poor father's sure got his hands full with that one!" And whenever there was anything that needed to be done, the elder one always had to do it. But when it was late in the day, or night had already fallen and the father wanted him to fetch something that forced him to pass in front of a graveyard or some other scary place, the elder son said, "Oh, no, Father, I won't go there, it gives me the creeps!" for he was fearful. Or when stories were told by the fire at night that made your skin crawl, he would often remark, "Lord, it gives me the willies!" But the younger son sat in his corner and had no idea what they were talking about. "People always say, It gives me the creeps, it gives me the willies! But nothing scares me – it's probably another thing I know nothing about."

One day the father said to him, "You there in your corner, you're getting big and strong, and it's time you learned something that'll let you earn your daily bread. See how your brother applies himself to everything he does, but with you, it's a lost cause."

"Oh, Father," he replied, "I would gladly learn something. If it's all right with you, I'd like to learn fear. That's something I just don't understand."

The elder son laughed out loud when he heard this, and thought to himself, Dear God, my brother is a hopeless case, he'll never amount to anything – as the twig is bent, so it grows.

The father sighed and said, "Fear, my son, is something you'll learn by and by, but you won't earn your bread with it."

Not long after that the sexton happened to drop by; the father poured out his heart to him and told him how his younger son was such a ne'er-do-well, he couldn't learn a thing. "Can you imagine, when I asked him how he hoped to earn his bread, he asked to learn fear."

"If that's your only worry," replied the sexton, "he can learn it from me. Just send him over, I'll set him straight."

The father was pleased, since he thought to himself, He'll sharpen that dull blade for me. So the sexton took the boy with him and had him ring the church bells. A few days later the sexton awakened him at midnight and told him to get up, climb the belfry, and ring the bells. You'll learn fear all right, he thought to himself, then snuck on ahead of him, and when the lad had climbed the tower and turned around, he saw a white figure standing before him on the steps opposite the resonance chamber.

"Who's there?" he called, but the figure made no reply and didn't stir or budge. "Answer me," cried the boy, "or begone. You have no business being here."

But the sexton didn't budge, so that the simpleton would think he was a ghost. The boy cried out a second time, "What business do you have here? Speak, if you're an honest man, or I'll throw you down the steps."

The sexton thought, He can't be serious. So he made no reply, and stood there as still as a stone.

Now the boy addressed him a third time, and when this too was to no avail, he lunged at him and shoved the ghost down the stairs, so that he landed in a corner ten steps below. Whereupon he calmly rang the bell, headed home, lay down without another word, and went back to sleep.

The sexton's wife waited a long time for her husband, but he didn't return. Finally she got frightened, woke the boy, and asked him, "Don't you know where my husband is? He climbed the belfry before you."

"No," replied the boy, "but I did see somebody standing on the stairs in front of the resonance chamber, and since he didn't answer when spoken to, and wouldn't go away, I took him for a thief and threw him down. Better go there and see if it was him or not. I'm awful sorry if it was."

The woman made haste and found her husband lying in a corner with a broken leg, wailing.

She helped him down the belfry steps, and then hurried off in a huff to have it out with the boy's father. "Your son," she yelled, "did a terrible thing. He threw my husband down the steps, so that he broke a leg – get that good-for-nothing out of our house!"

Horrified, the father came running over and bawled the boy out. "What a dumb-ass thing to do. The devil himself must have made you do it."

"But Father," the boy replied, "just listen, I'm completely innocent – he stood there in the dark like someone with evil intentions. I had no idea who it was, and warned him three times to speak up or begone."

"Dear God," said the father, "you bring me nothing but misfortune. Begone yourself, I don't want to see you again."

"Yes, Father, gladly I will. Just wait until daybreak, and I'll set out to learn fear, then at least I'll know something I can live on."

"Learn what you like," said the father, "it's all the same to me. Here, take these fifty pence to start you on your way. Go out into the world and don't tell a single soul where you come from and who your father is. You bring me nothing but shame."

"Yes, Father, as you wish. If that's all you ask, it's easy enough to do."

So at daybreak, the boy put the fifty pence in his pocket and set out on the highway, muttering to himself, "If only I knew fear! If only I knew fear!"

Then a man came along and heard what the boy said to himself, and after they'd walked for a while together and passed the gallows, the man said to him, "See over there, that's the tree where seven men got hitched up to the rope-maker's daughter and are now taking flying lessons – just sit yourself down there and wait for nightfall. You'll learn fear all right!"

"If there's nothing else to it," replied the lad, "that's simple enough. If I really learn fear so quickly, I'll give you my fifty pence. Just come back tomorrow morning."

So the boy went over to the gallows tree, sat down under it, and waited for night to fall. And since he felt chilly he lit himself a fire, but 'round about midnight the wind blew so cold even the fire couldn't keep him warm. And when the wind blew so hard, it made the hanged men knock against one another. He thought to himself, If you're freezing your behind off beside the fire, just imagine how cold and uncomfortable those fellas up there must be. And feeling sorry for them, he fetched a ladder, climbed up, and loosened the knot of one after another, taking all seven of them down. Whereupon he stoked the fire, blew on it, and set them around it so that they could warm themselves. But they just sat there and didn't budge, and their clothes caught fire. And he said, "Better watch out, boys, or I'll hang you back up." But the dead took no heed. They kept still and let their rags burn. So the boy got angry and said, "If you won't watch out for yourselves, there's nothing I can do to help you. I don't want to burn along with you." And one after the other, he hung them back up. Then he sat back down beside his fire and fell asleep.

And in the morning the man came by and wanted his fifty pence, and he said, "So now do you know what fear is?"

"No," the boy replied. "How was I supposed to learn it? Those fellas up there didn't open their mouths, and they were so stupid they let the old rags they had on burn off their backs."

The man saw that he was not going to get his fifty pence today, and he went off swearing, "Heaven help me, I've never seen such a piece of work."

So the boy continued on his way and started muttering to himself again, "If only I knew fear! If only I knew fear!"

A carter came walking up behind him, heard him muttering, and asked, "Who are you?"

"I don't know," the boy replied.

Then the carter asked, "Where are you from?"

"I don't know."

"What's your father's name?"

"I'm not supposed to say."

"What do you keep muttering to yourself?"

"Oh," the boy replied, "I want to learn fear, but nobody can teach it to me."

"Stop talking nonsense," the carter said. "Come along with me, I'll look after you."

So the boy went along with the carter, and that evening they came to an inn where they hoped to put up for the night. And once inside, the boy started muttering aloud to himself again, "If only I knew fear! If only I knew fear!"

Now the innkeeper heard it, laughed, and said, "If that's your pleasure, we can surely oblige."

"Pshaw!" said the innkeeper's wife. "Many a daredevil already forfeited his life. It'd be a pity and a shame for the boy's beautiful eyes if they never saw the light of day again."

But the young man said, "However hard it might be, I want to learn it once and for all. That's why I left home in the first place." He would not let up until the innkeeper told him that not far away stood a castle with a curse on it, where a fella could very well learn what fear is if only he managed to spend three nights inside standing guard. The king had promised his daughter's hand in marriage to anyone brave enough to try it, and she was said to be the most beautiful maiden the sun had ever shone on – and in the castle there was also a great treasure trove watched over by evil spirits, a treasure that would then be set free and was plentiful enough to make a poor man rich. Many had already tried their luck within, but not a single one ever came out again.

So the following morning, the boy went to the king and said, "By your leave, sire, I'd like to stand guard three nights in the cursed castle."

The king looked him over, and because he liked his face, he said, "You can ask for three things, but they must be lifeless things, to take with you into the castle."

To which the boy replied, "Then I ask for a fire, a lathe, and a carver's bench with a carving knife."

The king had everything the boy asked for taken to the castle by day. At twilight, the young man went in, lit himself a bright fire in an empty room, placed the lathe beside him, and sat down on the carver's bench. "If only I knew fear," he said aloud, "but I won't learn it here either."

At midnight he wanted to stoke his fire – but as he blew on it, there came a cry from the corner of the room: "Hell's bells, we're trembling with cold!"

"You fools," cried the boy, "what are you crying about? If you're cold you can sit by my fire and warm yourselves."

No sooner had he said it than a pair of big black cats bounded out of the dark with a mighty leap and sat themselves down beside him, eyeing him with their fiery eyes. After a little while, once they had warmed themselves, they said, "Well, friend, what do you say we play a game of cards?"

"Why not?" the boy replied. "But first show me your paws." So the cats extended their claws. "My," he said, "what long nails you have! Permit me to pare them for you." Whereupon he grabbed them by their necks, lifted them onto the lathe, and screwed down their paws. "I caught you red-handed," he said, "and it made me lose my appetite for cards!" Then he killed them and tossed them out into the moat.

But no sooner had he laid those two to rest and prepared to plunk himself back down beside his fire than black cats and black dogs came flying out from all directions, ever more and more of them, so that he couldn't ward them off – they whooped and howled something awful, stamped on his fire, pulling it apart, and tried to put it out. He looked on patiently for a while, but when things got out of hand he grabbed his carving knife and cried, "Get lost, you miserable lot!" and lunged at them. Some leapt aside, others he managed to kill and hurled their bodies out into the moat.

Upon his return he blew on the glowing embers, started his fire up again, and warmed himself. And as he sat there, his eyes wouldn't stay open, and he had a hankering for sleep. So he looked around and saw a big bed in the corner. "That's a sight for sore eyes," he said and lay himself down. But no sooner did he shut his eyes than the bed set itself in motion and hightailed it all over the castle. "Let's go then," he said, "full speed ahead." Then the bed rolled off as if it were drawn by six horses, through doorways and over steps, up and down – clippety-clop! – and all of a sudden it turned itself upside down, so that it was stacked like a mountain upon him. But he pried loose blankets and pillows, crawled out, and said, "Go fly off where you like, I'm tired," then lay himself down beside the fire and slept until daybreak.

The next morning the king came by, and when he saw the boy lying there on the ground he thought the evil spirits had done him in and he was dead. So he said, "Such a shame, he was a lovely person!"

The boy heard it, sat himself upright, and said, "Not so fast!"

Now the king was stunned, but happy to see him stir, and asked him how things had gone.

"Very well, thank you," the lad replied. "That's one night down and two to go." And when he went back to the innkeeper, the man could not believe his eyes.

"I never thought I'd see you again alive and kicking," he said. "Did you learn what fear is?"

"No," said the boy, "it's all for naught – if only somebody could set me straight!"

On the second night he returned to the old castle, sat himself down by the fire, and returned to muttering his old complaint: "If only I knew fear!" Come midnight a racket started up in the room, first softly, then louder and louder, then it was still again, and finally one half of a man came howling down the chimney and fell before him. "Hey there," the boy cried, "there's half of you missing." Then the awful racket started up again, the raving and roaring, and the other half of the man fell down. "Wait," said the boy, "let me first stoke the fire a little." No sooner had he done so than the two halves came together, and a ghastly man took his seat on the bench. "That wasn't the deal," said the boy, "the bench is mine." The man wanted to chase him away, but the boy would have none of it, gave him a mighty shove, and sat himself back down in his place. Then more men came tumbling down the chimney, one after the other; they gathered together nine bones and two skulls and started playing ninepins. The boy got a hankering to join in, and he said, "Can I play too?"

"Sure, if you've got the money to wager."

"I've got plenty of money," he replied, "but your balls aren't round enough." So he took the skulls, screwed them in his lathe, and pressed them into shape. "Now they'll roll better," he said, "up an' at 'em! Now let's have some fun!" He played along and lost some of his money, but at the strike of twelve everything disappeared before his eyes. He lay down and fell fast asleep.

The following morning the king came and inquired, "So how did it go this time?"

"I played ninepins," the boy replied, "and lost a penny or two."

"Weren't you afraid?"

"Not on your life," he said. "I had a ball. Oh, if only I knew fear."

The third night he sat himself down again on his bench and grumbled, "If only I knew fear!" When it got late, six big men came in carrying a coffin. Then the boy said, "By God, that must be my cousin who died a few days ago," waved his finger, and called out, "Come, little cousin, come!" The men set the coffin down on the ground and the boy went up to it and lifted the lid – a dead man lay stretched out in it. He felt his face, but it was cold as ice. "Just wait," he said, "I'll warm you up a little." He went to the fire, warmed his hands, and lay them on the face, but the dead man remained cold. Then he took him out of the coffin, sat himself down beside the fire, lay him on his lap, and rubbed his

arms to make the blood flow again. When that didn't work, it occurred to him that when two people lie in bed together they warm each other, so he brought him to the bed, pulled the covers up, and lay himself down beside him. After a while the dead man got warmed up and started moving around. Then the boy said, "See, cousin, imagine if I hadn't warmed you!"

Whereupon the dead man sat up and said, "Now I'm going to strangle you!"

"What?" said the boy. "Is that how you show your gratitude? Back in your box you go!" And he picked him up, flung him back into the coffin, and shut the lid. Then the six men came and carried him off again. "It's just no use," said the boy to himself. "I'm not going to learn fear here."

Then a man came in, he was bigger than all the others and looked awful. He was old and had a long white beard. "You poor fool," he cried out, "you're about to learn fear, prepare to die!"

"Not so fast," replied the boy. "If I'm to die, I have to be there to experience it."

"I'll see to that all right," said the fiend.

"Keep your shirt on, mister, don't puff up your chest. I'm at least as strong as you and a whole lot stronger."

"We'll see about that," said the old man. "If you're stronger than me, I'll let you live. Come on, let's give it a go."

So he led him down dark corridors to a blacksmith's fire, took an ax, and with a single blow sunk the anvil into the ground.

"That's nothing," said the boy and went over to the other anvil – the old man went over to watch with his white beard hanging down. Then the boy grabbed and swung the ax, split the anvil in a single blow, and managed to catch hold of the beard. "Now I've got you," said the boy, "and it's your turn to die." So he grabbed an iron bar and struck the old man until he whimpered and whined and begged him to stop, promising him great riches if he did. The boy pulled back the ax and let him loose.

Then the old man led him back to the castle and took him to a cellar with three chests full of gold, and said, "One chest belongs to the poor, one to the king, and the third one is yours."

At the stroke of midnight, the demon disappeared, and the boy found himself standing alone in the dark. "I'll find my way out all right," he said to himself, tapped around him, and found his way back to the room, where he fell asleep by the fire.

The next morning the king came by again and said, "So, have you finally learned fear?"

"No," he replied. "What's the big deal? My dead cousin dropped by, and so did a bearded old man, who took me down to the cellar and showed me a stash of gold, but nobody taught me what fear is."

Then spoke the king, "You freed the castle from its curse and so will have my daughter as your bride."

"That's all well and good," replied the boy, "but I still haven't learned what fear is."

So the gold was fetched and the wedding celebrated, but much as he loved his bride and glad as he was, the young king kept saying, "If only I knew fear, if only I knew fear." Which finally made the princess mad.

Her chambermaid said, "Permit me to help, milady. I'll teach him fear." She went out to the brook that flowed through the castle garden and fished out a bucketful of goldfish. And while the young king slept, she bid his wife pull back the blanket and shower him with a bucket of cold water and goldfish so that the little fish wriggled all over him. Whereupon he awakened with a cry: "Jeepers creepers, honey! By God, now I know what fear is."

THE DEVIL WITH THE THREE GOLDEN HAIRS

T*here once was* a poor woman who gave birth to a little son, and because he came into the world with a caul it was foretold of him that at age fourteen he would wed the daughter of a king. It so happened, shortly thereafter, that the king came to visit the village, but nobody knew it was the king, and when he asked the people for the latest news, they replied, "A few days ago a child was born with a caul. Good luck will shine on all his undertakings. It was foretold of him that in his fourteenth year he will take the king's daughter to wife."

The king, who had an evil heart and was displeased by the prophecy, went to the parents, pretending to be well-intentioned, and said, "You poor people, permit me to adopt your child, I will provide for all his needs." At first they hesitated, but seeing as the stranger offered them hard cash, they thought, Ours is a good-luck child, it must be for the best. They finally agreed and gave him the boy.

The king put the boy in a box and rode away with it, until he came to a deep body of water; then he tossed the box in and thought, I've saved my daughter from this unexpected suitor. But the box did not go under, it floated like a little boat, and not a drop of water leaked in. It floated to within two miles of the king's capital where it got stuck on the dam of a mill. A mill hand who fortunately happened to be present and noticed the box, pulled it out of the water with a long hook and thought he would find great riches, but when he opened the box, there inside lay a beautiful boy, bubbling with joy. He brought the boy back to the miller and his wife, and because they had no children they were overjoyed and said, "God blessed us with this boy." They took good care of the foundling and fed him well, and he grew up to be a fine and handsome lad.

It came to pass that the king once stopped at the mill during a thunderstorm and asked the miller and his wife if the tall, handsome lad was their son. "No," they replied, "he's a foundling. Fourteen years ago he came floating up in a box and a mill hand pulled him out of the water." Then the king realized that it was none other than the good-luck child whom he had tossed into the water, and said, "Good people, might the boy take a message back to the queen? I'll give him three gold pieces in payment."

"The king's wish is our command," they replied, and told the lad to get ready.

Whereupon the king wrote a letter to the queen that said, "As soon as the boy arrives bearing this letter, he is to be killed and buried, and all this must happen before I get back."

The boy set out with this letter in hand but got lost along the way and, come evening, arrived in a great forest. In the darkness he saw a little light, and drawing near, he came to a little house. He entered and found an old woman seated all alone by the fire. Frightened, she said, "Where do you come from and where are you going?"

"I come from the mill," he replied, "and am going to the queen to bring her a letter – but seeing as I got lost in the woods, I was wondering if I could spend the night here."

"You poor boy," said the woman, "this is a den of thieves, and if they find you here when they get home they will kill you."

"Come what may," said the boy, "I'm not afraid, but I'm so tired I can't walk another step," whereupon he lay himself down on a bench and fell fast asleep.

Not long thereafter the robbers got home and asked in a rage what this strange boy was doing lying there.

"Oh," said the old woman, "he's just an innocent child who got lost in the woods, and I took him in out of pity – he is on his way to the queen to bring her a letter."

The robbers opened the letter and read that as soon as he reached the palace, the boy bearing this letter was to be killed. Now the hard-hearted robbers took pity on the boy, and their leader tore up the letter and drafted another, in which it said that as soon as the boy arrived he was immediately to be married to the princess. They then let him sleep peacefully on the bench until morning, and when he awakened, they gave him the letter and showed him the right way to the royal residence. As soon as the queen opened and read the letter, she did what it said. She threw a sumptuous wedding feast, and the princess was married to the good-luck child; and since the youth was handsome and kind, she was glad and lived happily with him.

Some time later the king returned to the castle and saw that the prophecy had been fulfilled and that the good-luck child was wed to his daughter.

"How did this happen?" he asked. "My letter contained an altogether different command."

Then the queen handed him the letter and told him to read for himself what it said. The king read it and saw that his letter had been swapped with another.

He asked the youth what became of the letter he had entrusted to him, why he had brought another in its place.

"I have no idea," said the boy. "It must have been swapped with another as I slept in the forest."

Enraged, the king replied, "You won't get off that easy. Whoever wants to have my daughter must first fetch me three golden hairs from the Devil's own head in Hell. Bring me what I ask and you can keep my daughter." With this the king hoped to be rid of him forever.

But the good-luck child replied, "Gladly will I go fetch the three golden hairs. I'm not afraid of the Devil." Whereupon he took his leave and set out on his way.

The road led him to a great city, where the gatekeeper at the city gate asked him what trade he plied and what he knew.

"I know everything," replied the good-luck child.

"Then you can do us a favor," said the guard, "if you could tell us why our marketplace well which used to run deep with wine now no longer even gives us water."

"That I will find out for you," replied the youth. "Just wait till I return."

Then he continued on his way and came to another city, in which the gate-keeper once again asked him what trade he plied and what he knew.

"I know everything," he said.

"Then you can do us a favor and tell us why a tree in our town which used to bear golden apples now no longer even grows leaves."

"That I will find out for you," the youth replied. "Just wait till I return."

Then he continued on his way and came to a great body of water that he was obliged to cross. The ferryman asked him what trade he plied and what he knew.

"I know everything," he replied.

"Then you can do me a favor," said the ferryman, "and tell me why I must always ferry back and forth and never be relieved of my duty."

"That I will find out for you," the youth replied. "Just wait till I return."

Once he got to the other side of the body of water he found the gateway to Hell. It was black and sooty inside and the Devil was not home, but his grandmother sat there in an easy chair.

"What do you want?" she said to him, though she didn't look mean at all.

"I would like to have three golden hairs from the Devil's head," he replied, "or else I can't keep my wife."

"That's asking a lot," she said. "When the Devil gets home and finds you here, things won't go well for you, but I have pity on you. I'll see if I can help." She transformed him into an ant and said, "Crawl into the pleats of my skirt. You will be safe there."

"Right," he said, "but there are three things I'd still like to know: Why a well that once ran deep with wine has dried up and no longer even gives water; why a tree that once bore golden apples no longer even grows leaves; and why a ferryman has to keep ferrying back and forth and is never relieved of his duty."

"Those are difficult questions," she replied, "but just keep still, don't budge, and listen to what the Devil says when I pluck out the three golden hairs."

When night fell, the Devil came home. No sooner had he returned than he noticed that the air was not clean. "Something is not right," he said. "I smell the scent of human flesh." Then he searched every corner, but he couldn't find anything.

His grandmother scolded him. "I just swept the place," she said, "and made everything nice and tidy, and you have to go and make a mess again. You've always got the scent of human flesh in your nose! Sit down and eat your dinner." Once he had eaten and drunk, he felt tired, lay his head in his grandmother's lap, and asked her to delouse him a little. It didn't take long before he fell fast asleep, whistling and snoring. Then the old woman grabbed a golden hair, tore it out, and lay it beside her.

"Ouch!" cried the Devil. "What's the idea?"

"I had a troubled dream," his grandmother replied, "so I grabbed you by the hair."

"What did you dream?" asked the devil.

"I dreamed that a marketplace well that ordinarily ran deep with wine went dry and no longer even gave water. What do you suppose is the reason?"

"If only they knew!" the Devil replied. "There is a toad under a stone in the well. If they kill it, the wine will flow again."

His grandmother went on plucking lice until he fell asleep again and snored so loudly the windows rattled. Then she tore out a second hair.

"Hey! What's the idea?" cried the Devil in a rage.

"Don't take it badly," she replied. "I did it in my dream."

"What did you dream this time?" he asked.

"I dreamed of a fruit tree standing in a kingdom, which used to bear golden apples but now won't even grow a leaf. What do you suppose is the reason?"

"If only they knew!" the Devil replied. "A mouse is gnawing at the roots. If they kill the mouse, the tree will bear golden apples again, but if it keeps on gnawing, the tree will wither and die. But don't bother me any more with your dreams. If you disturb my sleep again I'll box your ears."

His grandmother calmed him down and went back to picking lice until he fell back asleep and snored. Then she grabbed the third golden hair and tore it out.

The Devil jumped up, hollered, and was about to strike her, but she managed to calm him down again and said, "I can't help it if I dream bad dreams!"

"What did you dream this time?" he asked, quite curious.

"I dreamed of a ferryman who complained that he had to keep ferrying back and forth and nobody ever took his place. What do you suppose is the reason?"

"That numskull!" replied the Devil. "If somebody comes by and wants to be ferried across, he's got to hand the other man the pole, then the other is stuck ferrying and he is free to go."

Once the grandmother had plucked out the three golden hairs and made the old Devil answer the three questions, she left him in peace and he slept until daybreak.

As soon as the Devil had departed, the old woman plucked the ant out of a pleat in her skirt and gave the good-luck child his human form back. "Here are your three golden hairs," she said. "You heard for yourself what the Devil said in answer to your questions."

"Yes," he replied, "I heard it and will remember it."

"Happy to have been of assistance," she said. "So now you can continue on your way."

He thanked the old woman for her help in a pinch, left Hell behind, and was glad that everything had worked out so well. Once he came to the ferryman, it was time to pass on the promised reply. "First ferry me across," said the good-luck child, "then I'll tell you how you can save yourself." And once he'd reached the far shore, he gave the ferryman the Devil's advice: "The next time somebody comes by and asks to be ferried across, just hand him the pole."

Then he kept on walking and came to the city with the sterile tree, where the gatekeeper had also sought a reply. He told the gatekeeper the Devil's advice: "Kill the mouse that's gnawing at the roots, and the tree will bear golden apples again." The gatekeeper thanked him and as a reward gave him two donkeys loaded with gold to follow him on his way.

Finally he came to the city with the well that had run dry. Then he told the guard what the Devil had said: "There's a toad in the well hiding under a stone.

Find it and kill it and the well will once again bubble with wine." The guard thanked him and gave him another two donkeys loaded with gold.

At last the good-luck child got home to his wife, who rejoiced to see him again and to hear that everything had gone well. He brought the king the Devil's three golden hairs he had asked for, and when the king saw the four donkeys loaded with gold he was glad and said, "Now that all my demands have been fulfilled you can keep my daughter. But, my dear son-in-law, do tell me where you got all that gold. It's quite a treasure trove!"

"I crossed a river," the good-luck child replied, "and that's where I picked it up. The shoreline on the other side is strewn with gold instead of sand."

"Can I get myself some too?" asked the king with greedy glee.

"As much as you want," the lad replied. "There's a ferryman by the river. Just ask him to carry you across, and you can fill your bags on the other side."

The avaricious king went as fast as he could, and when he came to the river he waved to the ferryman to take him across. The ferryman came and asked him to climb in, and as soon as they reached the far shore he passed him the pole and leapt ashore. And from then on the king had to keep ferrying back and forth for his sins.

"Is he still at it?"

"What do you think? Who would have been fool enough to let him pass them the pole?"

THE BRAVE LITTLE TAILOR

One summer morning a little tailor sat contented at his table by the window, sewing up a storm. Then a peasant woman came walking down the street and called out, "Good jam for sale! Good jam for sale!"

The little tailor liked the sound of it, so he poked his wisp of a head out the window and called to her: "Up here, good woman, you can load it off on me."

The woman lugged her heavy basket the three flights up to the tailor's place and unpacked all her pots before him. He looked them over, picked them up, practically planted his nose in the sweet stuff, and finally said, "The jam looks delicious. Dish me out four ounces, good woman, and if it comes to a quarter pound, I don't mind." The woman, who had hoped to sell him a considerable amount, gave him what he asked for but went away grim-faced and grumpy. "Let this jam be blessed by God," prayed the tailor, "and let it give me force and strength," whereupon he proceeded to fetch a loaf of bread from the cupboard, cut himself a slice, and spread it with the jam. "It will sweeten my day," he said, "but first let me finish sewing my jacket before I take a bite."

So he lay the slice of bread beside him, kept on sewing, and feeling giddy

with joy, sewed larger and larger stitches. Meanwhile the scent of the sweet jam wafted up the wall, where flies gathered in ever greater number, and lured below, swarms of them pounced on it. "Hey, who invited you to the table?" said the tailor and swished away his uninvited guests. But the flies, who understood no German, would not let themselves be dissuaded from dining, returning in ever greater numbers. Finally the tailor was, as they say, at his wit's end, so he fetched a flyswatter from a drawer, and muttering "Here's your just dessert!" came down with a merciless swat. When he lifted the swatter and counted his quarry, no less than seven lay there with outstretched legs. "Well, will you get a load of that!" he said, admiring his prowess. "I'm gonna let the whole town know!" So the little tailor hastily cut himself a belt, and stitched and embroidered a logo on the leather in big letters: "Seven with one blow!" "Never mind the city!" he cheered himself on, "I'm going to let the whole world know!" And his heart beat for joy in his breast like a little lamb's tail.

The tailor bound the belt around his waist and decided to go out into the world, for he felt that his workshop was just too small for such prowess as his. Before leaving, he looked around to see if there was anything he might take along, but all he found was an old hunk of cheese, which he thought might come in handy. Outside, in front of his door, he noticed a bird caught in a bush, and he packed it along with the cheese.

Whereupon he bravely sallied forth, and being light and nimble, he felt no fatigue. The path led him up a mountain, and when he reached the summit there sat a mighty giant taking his ease. Feeling feisty, the little tailor went right up to him, greeted him, and said, "Splendid day, isn't it, my friend, to sit around surveying the big, wide world! I've just set out to try my luck. Would you like to come along?"

The giant eyed the tailor with disdain and said, "You worm! You miserable wretch!"

"That does it!" replied the little tailor, then unbuttoned his jacket and showed the giant his belt. "You can read with your own eyes what kind of stuff I'm made of."

The giant read "Seven with one blow," figured it meant seven men felled by the tailor, and felt a modicum of respect for the little fellow. Still, he wanted to put him to the test, and taking a stone in hand, pressed it hard until the water dripped out. "Do as I did," said the giant, "if you're strong enough."

"Is that all?" said the tailor. "That's child's play!" He shrugged, reached in his pocket, fetched out the hunk of soft cheese, and pressed it until the whey dripped out. "Well what do you think of that!"

The giant was speechless, unable to believe his eyes. Then he picked up a stone and hurled it so high you could hardly still see it. "All right, little munchkin, match that!"

"Not bad," said the tailor, "but the stone fell back down to earth again. I'll hurl one that'll never fall down." He reached into his pocket, grabbed the bird, and tossed it into the air. Happy to have found its freedom again, the bird took flight and didn't come back. "What do you think of that, pal!" said the tailor.

"You can throw all right," replied the giant, "but let's see what you can lift." So he led the tailor to a mighty oak tree felled and lying flat on the ground. "If you've got the muscle, help me carry the tree out of the forest."

"Gladly," replied the little man. "You take the trunk on your shoulders, and I'll carry the branches and all the leaves, that's the most cumbersome part."

The giant lifted the trunk onto his shoulders, but the tailor sat himself on a branch, and being unable to turn around, the giant had to carry the entire tree and the tailor on top of it. Meanwhile, in cheerful spirits, the tailor made merry in back, whistling the ditty "Three tailors rode out through the gate . . ." as if carrying the tree were a matter of child's play. After hauling the heavy load for a while, the giant was beat and called out, "Listen, I've got to let the tree drop." The tailor leapt nimbly to the ground, grabbed hold of the branches with both his hands, as though he'd been carrying it, and said to the giant, "You're such a big fellow and can't even hold up your own end."

They continued on their way together, and when they passed a cherry tree, the giant gripped the top of the tree where the ripest cherries hung, bent it down, and beckoned the tailor to grab hold and eat of them. But the little tailor was much too weak to hold down the tree, and when the giant let go, the tree flew back up and catapulted the tailor head over heels into the air. As soon as he dropped down again without a scratch, the giant said, "Where's you muscle, man? Have you not strength enough to hold down that little riding crop?"

"It's not for lack of strength," replied the little tailor. "Do you really think a man who felled seven with one blow couldn't attend to such a trifle? I leapt over the tree because the hunters down there in the bushes are shooting. Do as I did, if you dare."

The giant gave it a try, but unable to clear the top of the tree, he got caught in the branches, so that in this, too, the tailor had the upper hand.

Then the giant said, "If you're such a brave buck, come with me to our cave and spend the night with us." The little tailor agreed and followed him. When they reached the cave they found other giants seated by the fire, and each had a roast sheep in hand and ate of it. The little tailor looked around and thought, It's a lot roomier here than in my workshop. The giant pointed to a bed and said the little tailor could rest his weary bones in it, but the bed was too big for the little tailor, so he didn't lay himself down in it but crept into a corner. Come midnight, the giant thought the little tailor must be fast asleep, so he got up, took a big iron bar, and struck the bed with such a heavy blow he thought for sure he had flattened that grasshopper. At the crack of dawn the giants went into the forest and completely forgot about the tailor, but all of a sudden the little man came cheerfully and defiantly walking up to them. The giants trembled, afraid he would kill them all, and ran for their lives.

The tailor continued on his way, following the tip of his nose. After walking a long while he came to the courtyard of a royal palace, and because he was tired he lay himself down in the grass and fell asleep. As he slept, people came by, looked him over from every angle, and read the slogan on his belt: "Seven with one blow."

"Forsooth," they said, "what does such a great warrior want among us here in peacetime? He must be a mighty fighter." So they went and reported his presence to the king, thinking that if war should break out he would surely be an important and valuable ally to be retained at any price. The king approved of such advice, and sent one of his courtiers to the little tailor to wait for him to wake up and propose that he serve the king's force. The emissary stood by the sleeper, waited until he stretched his limbs and batted his eyes open, whereupon he made his offer.

"That is precisely why I came," the tailor replied. "I am ready and willing to serve the king." So he was received with great honors and assigned a splendid apartment.

The gentlemen of the army, however, were wary of the little tailor and wished him a thousand miles away. "What will come of it?" they grumbled among themselves. "If we get into a spat with him and he lashes out, seven of us will fall with one blow. We mere mortals won't survive it." So they came to a decision. They all went to see the king and asked him to release them from service. "We just haven't got it in us," they said, "to measure up against a man who can fell seven with one blow."

The king regretted forfeiting all his faithful fighters on account of one warrior. He wished he'd never set his eyes upon him and wanted to be rid of him again. But he did not dare give him his walking papers, as he feared the fellow might slaughter him along with all his people and set himself on the throne. After pondering long and hard, he finally had an idea. He sent word to the little tailor and told him that, because he was such a great war hero, he wanted to make him an offer. In his realm there lived two giants who wreaked havoc with looting, murder, arson, and such; no one dared face them at the risk of his life. If he could prevail and lay them low, he would be given the king's only daughter as a bride and half the kingdom as a dowry, and he would have a hundred cavalrymen as reinforcements.

That would be something for a guy like me, thought the little tailor. It isn't every day you're offered a pretty princess and half a kingdom. "Very well," he replied, "I'll put those giants in their place, and I don't need the help of a hundred cavalrymen to do it – he who can fell seven with one blow needn't worry about two."

So the little tailor set out and the hundred cavalrymen followed him. When he got to the edge of the forest, he said to his retinue, "You just stay here, I'll make short shrift of the giants on my own." Then he leapt into the forest and peered to the right and to the left. A little while later he spotted the two giants – they lay asleep under a tree, snoring so hard the branches bent up and down. Without dawdling, the little tailor filled both his pockets with stones and climbed the tree. Once he'd reached the middle, he slipped down a branch, until he was seated directly over the sleepers, and let fall one stone after another on the chest of one of the giants. For the longest time the giant felt nothing, but finally he woke up, poked his partner, and said, "Why are you hitting me?"

"You're dreaming," said the other. "I haven't touched you."

As soon as they went back to sleep, the tailor tossed stones down on the second giant.

"What's the idea!" the latter cried out. "Why are you throwing things at me?"

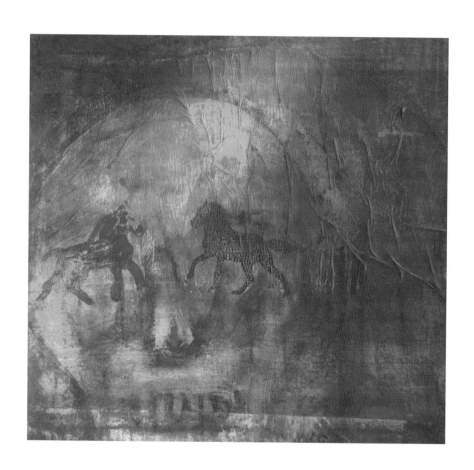

"I'm not throwing anything at you," the other grumbled.

They squabbled for a while, but seeing as they were tired, they soon made up and their eyes fell shut again. Then the little tailor began his game again. He searched for the heaviest stone he could find and hurled it with all his might at the chest of the first giant.

"That does it!" he cried, and leaping up like a lunatic, shoved his partner so hard against the tree trunk that it trembled. The other giant responded in like manner, and they got so angry they tore up trees and pummeled each other until finally both lay dead on the ground. Whereupon the little tailor leapt down from his perch. "Lucky thing," he said, "they didn't tear up the tree in which I sat, or else I would have had to leap like a squirrel to another tree – but a guy like me has got to stay on his toes!" He pulled out his sword and dealt each of the giants a mighty stroke in the chest, whereupon he went back to the cavalrymen and reported, "The job is done, I finished them both off. Though they put up a fight and tore up trees to defend themselves, it was no use against a guy like me who can fell seven with one blow."

"Aren't you even wounded?" asked the cavalrymen.

"Not a scratch," replied the tailor. "They didn't ruffle a hair on my head."

The cavalrymen did not want to believe him and rode into the forest. There they found the giants bathed in blood, and 'round about them lay the uprooted trees.

So the little tailor demanded his just reward from the king, who, however, regretted his promise and pondered how to get rid of the hero. "Before you can get my daughter and half of my kingdom," said the king, "you must still accomplish one more heroic act. In the forest there is a unicorn running wild and wreaking havoc. You've got to catch it first."

"I'm far less afraid of a unicorn than of two giants. Seven with one blow, that's my motto."

The little tailor took along an ax and a rope and went to the forest, and again he told his retinue to wait for him. He didn't have to search for long before the unicorn came charging right at him as though it meant to spear him through with a single thrust.

"Not so fast," he said, "you'll have to do better than that." Then he stood stock-still, waited until the beast was almost upon him, whereupon he spryly leapt behind a tree. The unicorn ran with all its might against the tree and got its horn stuck so fast in the trunk that it didn't have the strength to pull it out again, and so was trapped. "Now I've got the bird in the bag," said the tailor, stepping forth from behind the tree. First he tied the rope around the unicorn's neck, then with a heave of his ax cut the horn from the tree, and once he was done he led the creature and brought it before the king.

But the king would still not grant him the promised reward and made a third demand. Before the wedding could take place the tailor had to catch the wild boar that was wreaking havoc in the forest. The king's hunters would lend him a hand.

"Gladly," said the tailor. "That's child's play."

The little tailor did not take the hunters with him into the forest, and they were right pleased about that, for the wild boar had already more than once welcomed them with its tusks, so that they had no desire to stalk it. When the boar spotted the tailor, it lunged at him with foaming mouth and gnashing teeth and wanted to mow him down, but the fleet-footed hero slipped inside a chapel that stood nearby and promptly leapt back out a window. The boar ran in after him, but the little tailor hopped to it outside and slammed the door shut behind the boar, and being much too heavy and cumbersome to jump out the window, the seething beast was trapped inside. The little tailor called for the hunters to come see the captive creature with their own eyes, while the hero made tracks to the king, who now, whether he wanted to or not, had to keep his promise and hand over his daughter and half his kingdom. Had he known that it was no war hero but a lowly little tailor standing there before him, he would have regretted it even more. The wedding was held with great pomp and little joy, whereupon the tailor became a king.

Some time after that the young queen overheard her husband muttering aloud in his sleep, "Better sew my vest, son, and patch up my pants, or I'll box your ears with this yardstick!" from which she surmised the young man's humble origins, of which she complained the next morning to the king, asking him to help her separate from this fellow who was nothing but a lowly tailor.

The king comforted her and said, "Leave your bedroom door open tonight. My servants will stand outside, and once he's asleep, they'll sneak in, tie him up, and put him on a ship bound for some far distant shore."

She was pleased with the plan, but the king's standard-bearer, who had overheard everything and was kindly disposed to the young man, revealed the entire plot to him.

"I'll nip that plan in the bud," said the little tailor.

That evening he went to bed with his wife at the regular time. Once she thought he was asleep, she got up, opened the door, and went back to bed. But the little tailor, who only pretended to be asleep, started clamoring, "Better sew my vest, son, and patch up my pants, or I'll box your ears with this yardstick! I felled seven with one blow, slew two giants, ensnared a unicorn, and trapped a wild boar, and those waiting outside my bedroom door think I'm afraid of them!" When the king's servants heard this, they were overcome by fear, and not a one of them dared draw near. So the little tailor held on to his crown and remained a king for the rest of his life.

THE FROG KING,
OR IRON HENRY

In olden times, when wishing still worked, there lived a king whose daughters were all beautiful, but the youngest was so lovely that the sun itself that had seen so much was stunned every time it cast its rays on her face. Not far from the king's castle there was a deep, dark woods, and in the woods under an old linden tree, there was a spring. At the hottest time of the day the king's lovely child was wont to venture out into the woods and sit on the edge of the cool spring – and when she didn't know what to do, she took a golden ball, tossed it up in the air, and caught it again, and that was her favorite plaything.

It came to pass on one occasion that the golden ball did not drop into her open hands but fell short, struck the ground, and rolled right into the water. The king's daughter followed it with her eyes, but the ball disappeared, and the spring was deep, so deep you couldn't see the bottom. And she started crying, and kept crying louder and louder. She was beside herself with sadness.

Whereupon, in answer to her tears, a voice cried out, "What's the matter, princess? Your tears make even a stone take pity."

Looking around to see where the voice came from, she spotted a frog poking his thick ugly head up out of the water. "Oh, it's you, old splatterpuss," she said. "I'm crying on account of my golden ball that fell into the spring."

"Be still and cry no more," replied the frog, "I might be able to help. But what will you give me if I bring back your precious plaything?"

"I'll give you whatever you want, dear frog," she said, "my clothes, my pearls and precious stones, and even the golden crown on my head."

To which the frog replied, "I couldn't give a hoot about your clothes, your pearls and precious stones, nor even your golden crown, but if you'll take me to heart, let me be your bosom friend and playmate, let me sit beside you at your little table, eat from your little golden plate, drink from your little cup, sleep in your little bed – if you promise to do that, then I'll dive down and bring up your golden ball."

"Oh, yes," she said, "I promise to do everything you wish, if you bring me back my golden ball." But she thought to herself, Foolish frog, what nonsense he blabbers! He floats and croaks among his own kind in the water and can't very well cavort with a human being.

But no sooner did she agree than the frog poked his head in the water and dove down, and a little while later came paddling back up with the ball in his mouth and flung it on the grass. The princess, overjoyed to see her splendid plaything again, picked it up and ran off with it.

"Wait, wait," cried the frog, "take me with you. I can't run as fast as you!"

But what good did it do him to croak after her as loud as he could! She wasn't listening. She hurried on home and promptly forgot the poor little frog, who had to hop back into its spring.

The next day while she sat at the table with the king and all his courtiers and

ate from her little golden plate, splitter-splat, splitter-splat, something came creeping up the marble steps, and once it reached the top, it knocked on the door and called out, "Little princess, let me in!"

She ran to see who it was outside, but when she opened the door she spotted the frog. So she slammed the door shut and went back to her seat at the table, trembling with fear. The king noticed that her heart was beating fast, and said, "My child, what's the matter? Is there a giant at the door who wants to drag you off?"

"Oh, no," she replied, "it's no giant, just a disgusting frog."

"What does the frog want from you?"

"Oh, Father dear, yesterday, when I sat by the spring in the forest playing with my golden ball, it fell into the water. And hearing me crying bitterly, the frog dove down and fetched it, and since he insisted, I promised he could be my mate, but I never thought he'd be able to wiggle his way out of the water. So now he's waiting outside and wants to come in."

Then the frog started knocking again and cried:

"Little princess, let me in,
Don't you recall
What you said by the spring
When you lost your ball,
Your favorite plaything?
Little princess, let me in!"

Then the king said, "A promise is a promise. Go now and let him in."

So she went and opened the door, and the frog hopped in and followed hot on her heels all the way to her little chair. He sat there and said, "Pick me up, princess." She hesitated, until finally the king made her do as the frog asked. And once he was on her chair, he wanted to be put on the table, and no sooner was he seated there than he said, "Now push your little golden plate toward me, so that we may eat together," which she did, though you could tell she didn't do it gladly. The frog ate with gusto, but every bite the princess took stayed stuck in her pretty throat. Finally he said, "I've eaten my fill and now I'm tired. Take me to your little room and fold down your silken bedcover. We'll take a little nap together."

The king's daughter started crying, afraid of the cold frog, whom she didn't dare touch and who now wanted to sleep in her clean and lovely little bed.

But the king got angry and said, "You dare not scorn him now, he who helped you when you were in need." Then he grabbed the frog with two fingers, carried him upstairs, and set him in a corner of her room. But when she lay in bed, the frog came crawling over and said, "I'm tired, princess, and want to sleep just like you do – pick me up or I'll tell your father."

Whereupon she flew into a bitter rage, picked him up, and flung him against the wall with all her might. "Enough is enough, you disgusting frog!"

But when he fell down, he was a frog no more, but a prince with beautiful and friendly eyes. And by her father's will they were wed. Then he told her how a witch had cast an evil spell on him, and nobody could have freed him from the spring but she alone. Tomorrow, he said, they would ride back to his realm.

Then they fell asleep, and the next morning when they were awakened by the first rays of sunlight, a carriage came rolling up drawn by eight white horses with peacock feathers on their heads, attached by golden chains, and in the coachman's box sat the young king's servant, Faithful Henry. Faithful Henry was so upset to see his master turned into a frog that he'd had three iron bands strung around his heart so that it wouldn't burst in pain and sorrow. The carriage had come to take the young king back to his kingdom. Faithful Henry lifted them both into the rig and climbed back into the coachman's box, overjoyed at the prince's deliverance from the evil spell. And after they'd driven for a while, the prince heard a crack, as though something had broken. So he turned around and cried: "Henry, the wagon's breaking."

"No, sire, it's my heart no longer aching,

A band has burst

To see you no more cursed,

The frog's hide you shed

When the princess took you to bed."

Again, and then again, something cracked along the way, and each time the prince thought it was the wagon breaking, but it was just the bands around Faithful Henry's heart bursting to see his master at last released from the spell, hale and happy with his lovely bride.

THE WHITE SNAKE

Long, long ago there lived a king renowned far and wide for his wisdom. There was nothing he didn't know about, and it was as if the knowledge of the most obscure things were reported to him through thin air. But he had one curious custom. Every day after the midday meal, when all the dishes were cleared from the table and everyone else had dispersed, a trusted servant had to bring him a bowl. But it was covered with a lid and even the servant had no idea what it contained, and not a soul knew the secret, for the king would not lift the lid and eat from it until he was all alone. This had been going on for quite some time, when, one day, as soon as the king was done, while carrying off the bowl, curiosity got the better of the servant, who brought the bowl to his room. Once he had locked the door behind him, he lifted the lid and saw a white snake curled up in the bottom of the bowl. As soon as he caught sight of it he could not resist the temptation to take a bite, so he cut off a little piece and put it in his mouth. But no sooner did it touch his tongue than he heard outside the window a strange whispering of faint voices. He poked his head out the window and pricked up his ears, and fathomed that it was the sparrows chattering, telling each other all that they had witnessed flying over field and forest. That snippet of snake had granted him the ability to understand the language of animals.

It so happened that on that very day the queen lost her loveliest ring, and suspicion fell on the trusted servant who had privileged access to every corner of the castle. The king called for him, and giving him a good tongue-lashing, threatened that if he could not find the thief by the following morning, then he himself would bear the guilt and be executed. It did the servant no good to swear to his innocence, the die was cast. In his angst and distress, he went walking up and down the castle grounds pondering how to get out of the mess he was in. He noticed a flock of ducks bobbing peacefully side by side in a bubbling brook, polishing their beaks, engaged in an intimate conversation. The servant stood still and listened in. They told each other where they had been waddling that morning and what tasty morsels they had managed to snap up, whereupon one remarked grumpily, "I've got something hard stuck in my gut. While nibbling away, in my haste I gobbled up and swallowed a ring lying under the queen's window."

Thereupon the servant grabbed the duck by the neck, carried her into the kitchen, and said to the cook, "Slaughter this one, she's good and fat."

"Right," said the cook, "she's good and fat and ready to be roasted." He cut the duck by the throat, and once she was served and carved up the queen's ring was found in her gut. So the servant could easily prove his innocence before the king, and since His Majesty wanted to make amends for his unjust accusation, he bid him request a favor and seek for himself the most respected position at court.

The servant refused all the king's offers, asking only for a horse and travel money, for he had a hankering to see the world and to spend some time kicking about. As soon as his wish was granted he set out, and one day he rode past a pond in which he noticed three fishes caught in the reeds and panting for water. Although it is said that fish are dumb, he immediately fathomed their lament at having to die in such a miserable way. Since he had a big heart, he promptly dismounted from his horse and released the three captives back into the water. They flounced about for joy, raised their heads, and called to him, "We will remember and repay your kindness at having saved us!"

He rode on and after a little while it seemed to him as if he heard a voice in the sand at his feet. He listened and overheard the complaint of an ant king: "If only people with their clumsy animals would watch where they're going! That dumb horse with its heavy hooves is mercilessly stomping my subjects to death!" Whereupon the sympathetic rider steered his horse down a side path, and the ant king called out to him, "We will remember and repay your kindness!"

The path led into a forest, and there he saw a raven father and raven mother perched beside their nest, flinging the baby birds out. "Away with you, you good-for-nothing brood," they cried. "We can't feed you any longer, and you're big enough now to fend for yourselves!"

The poor little ones lay on the ground fluttering and flapping their downy wings and crying, "You want us helpless baby birds to fend for ourselves, and we don't even know how to fly! What else can we do, but die of hunger?"

So the kindhearted youth dismounted, killed his horse with his dagger, and left its carcass to feed the baby ravens. They came hopping over, ate their fill, and cried, "We will remember and repay your kindness!"

Now he had to use his own two legs, and after walking a good long while he came to a big city. There was a hubbub and the streets were thronged with people, when a town crier came riding up and announced that the king's daughter was seeking a husband, but whoever asks for her hand in marriage must first accomplish a difficult task, and if he does not succeed it will cost him his life. Many had already tried but lost their lives in the process. When the young man saw the princess, he was so bedazzled by her great beauty that he forgot all the perils involved and presented himself before the king as a suitor.

No sooner did he do so than he was ferried out to sea, and before his eyes a golden ring was tossed in. Then the king bid him fetch that ring from the bottom of the sea and added: "If you come back up without the ring you will be tossed in the sea again and again until you drown."

Everyone pitied the handsome youth and left him alone on the beach. He stood by the shore and pondered what to do, when all of a sudden he saw three fishes come swimming over, and they were none others than the ones whose lives he had saved among the reeds. The middle fish held a mussel in its mouth, which it dropped in the sand at the young man's feet, and when the young man picked it up and opened it, the golden ring lay there in the shell. Overjoyed, the youth took the ring to the king, expecting to be granted the promised reward.

But upon learning that he was not her equal by birth, the haughty princess spurned him and demanded that he would first have to accomplish a second task. She went out to the garden and herself strewed ten sacks of millet in the grass. "By sun-up tomorrow morning, he must have finished gathering it all up," she said, "and not a grain may be missing."

The young man sat himself down in the garden and pondered how in heaven's name to fulfill such a charge, but he could think of nothing and so sat there sadly waiting for daybreak, when he would be led to his death. But when the first rays of sunlight fell on the garden, he saw the ten sacks of grain all lying stuffed side by side and not a grain was missing. The king of the ants had come with his army of thousands and thousands of ants and the grateful creatures had taken great pains to gather and bag all the grain. The princess herself came down to the garden and was stunned to see that the youth had accomplished the task he had been assigned, but she could not yet quell her proud heart and said, "Even though he managed to complete the two tasks, he will not become my husband until he brings me an apple from the tree of life."

The youth did not know where to find the tree of life. He set off and wanted to keep walking as long as his legs held out, but he had no hope of finding it. After he had traversed three kingdoms and, come evening, arrived at a forest, he sat himself under a tree and wanted to sleep, when he heard a fluttering in the branches, and a golden apple fell into his hand. Whereupon three ravens flew down to him, sat themselves on his knees, and said, "We are the three young ravens you saved from the jaws of hunger. When we grew up and heard that you were searching for the golden apple, we flew over the sea to the end of the earth where the tree of life stands and fetched you an apple."

Overjoyed, the young man made his way back to the city and brought the golden apple to the lovely princess, who now had no excuse to reject him. They shared the apple of life and both bit in and ate it, whereupon her heart was filled with love for him, and they found happiness and reached a ripe old age together.

THE QUEEN OF THE BEES

O*nce upon a time* two princes went out in search of adventure and led such a wild and dissolute life that they couldn't find their way home again. The third and youngest one, known as Simpleton, went in search of his brothers. But when he finally found them, they heaped him with scorn, saying that given his simplicity he shouldn't even try to make his way in the world, seeing as the two of them who were much smarter couldn't make it. So the three set out together and came to an anthill. The two elder brothers wanted to destroy it and watch the little ants running around in terror and carrying off their eggs, but Simpleton said, "Leave the creatures in peace. I can't abide your bothering them."

So they continued on their way and came to a lake in which many, many ducks were swimming around. The two elder brothers wanted to catch a few and roast them, but Simpleton wouldn't hear of it and said, "Leave the creatures in peace. I can't abide your killing them."

Finally they came to a beehive in a tree full of so much honey that it dripped down the trunk. The two elder brothers wanted to light a fire in front of the tree so that they could suffocate the bees and take their honey. But Simpleton stopped them again and said, "Let the creatures be. I can't abide your burning them."

At last the three brothers came to a castle. In its stables stood stone horses and there was not a living soul in sight. They went through all the rooms and halls until at the end of a corridor they saw a door with two locks. But in the middle of the door there was a small slit, through which they could peak into the room. Seated at a table they spied a little gray man. They called to him once, twice, but he did not hear them; they called a third time and he finally stood up, opened the locks, and came out. He did not say a word but led them to a richly laden table, and once they had eaten and drunk their fill, he brought each of them to his own bedroom.

The next morning the little gray man came to the eldest brother, winked, and led him to a stone tablet on which three tasks were inscribed whose completion would lead to the spell on the castle being lifted. The first task was: In the woods beneath the moss lay the pearls of the princess, a thousand in number, which had to be gathered, and if, come dusk, even a single one was missing, he who searched for them would turn to stone. The eldest brother went to the woods and searched all day, but by sundown he had only gathered a hundred. Just as the tablet said, he was turned to stone.

The following day the second brother undertook the same task, but he didn't do much better than the eldest. He found no more than two hundred pearls and was turned to stone.

At last it was Simpleton's turn. He searched in the moss, but it was so difficult to find the pearls and so slow. He sat himself down on a stone and started crying. And as he sat there, the king of the ants, whose life he had once saved, came with five thousand of his kind, and it wasn't long before the little creatures had found all the pearls and piled them in a heap.

The second task was to fetch the key to the princess's bedroom from the bottom of the lake. When Simpleton came to the lake, the ducks whose lives he had once saved came swimming up, dove down, and fetched the key from the depths.

But the third task was the hardest: From among the three sleeping princesses he was to select the youngest and dearest. But they all looked alike and had no distinguishing features, except that before falling asleep they had each consumed different sweets: the eldest a bag of sugar, the second a little syrup, the youngest a spoonful of honey. Then the queen of the bees whom Simpleton had saved from the fire came flying by and buzzed around the mouths of all three, but finally she landed on the mouth of the one who had eaten the honey, and so the prince recognized the right one. Whereupon the spell was lifted, all in the castle awakened from sleep, and whoever had been turned to stone came back to life. And Simpleton married the youngest and dearest and became king after her father's death, but his two brothers wed the other two sisters.

THE DRUMMER

One evening, a young drummer went walking alone in a field and came to a lake, on the shore of which he saw three strips of white linen lying about. "What fine linen!" he said to himself and put one strip in his pocket. He went home, giving no further thought to his find, and feeling tired, lay down in his bed. But just as he was about to fall asleep it seemed to him as if someone called out to him by name.

He pricked up his ears and heard a quiet voice whispering to him, "Drummer, drummer, wake up!"

Dark as it was, he could not see anyone, but it seemed to him as if a presence wafted about his bed. "What do you want?" he asked.

"Give me back my chemise that you took from me yesterday evening by the lake," the voice replied.

"You can have it," said the drummer, "if you tell me who you are."

"Oh," said the voice, "I am the daughter of a mighty king, but I was taken captive by an evil witch who holds me in her thrall on Glass Mountain. Every day I must bathe in the lake with my two sisters, but without my chemise I cannot fly away again. My sisters escaped but I had to remain behind. I beg you to give me back my chemise."

"Don't worry, poor child," said the drummer, "I'll gladly give it back."

He plucked it out of his pocket and handed it to her in the dark. She grabbed it from him and wanted to rush off.

"Wait a minute," he said, "perhaps I can help you."

"You can only help me if you climb Glass Mountain and free me from the witch's spell. But you'll never make it to Glass Mountain, and even if you manage to draw near, you won't be able to climb it."

"Where there's a will, there's a way," said the drummer. "I feel for you and fear nothing. But I don't know the way."

"The way leads through the great forest in which the man-eating ogres live," she replied. "More than that I may not tell." Whereupon he heard her whisk away.

At daybreak the drummer awakened, hung his drum around his neck, and fearlessly entered the forest. Once he had walked for a while and encountered no giant, he thought to himself, Better wake that lazybones! Then he grabbed his drum and drumsticks and struck up such a storm that the birds flew out of the trees with a great caw. Not long after that, a giant who had been lying asleep in the grass got up, and he was as tall as a fir tree. "Miserable wretch," he cried out, "why did you drum me out of the sweetest sleep?"

"I'm drumming," he replied, "to signal the way to the thousands of soldiers following me."

"What do they want in my forest?" asked the giant.

"They want to skin your hide and rid the forest of your monstrous lot."

"Oho," said the giant, "I'll trample on you like I trample on ants."

"You really think you can fight against thousands?" the drummer replied. "As soon as you grab for one he'll leap aside and hide, but when you lie down and fall asleep they'll creep out of the bushes, climb your sorry carcass, and make short shrift of you. Each soldier has a steel hammer dangling from his belt, and with it they'll crack your skull."

The giant grew sullen and thought, If I lock horns with that sly lot, things might turn out badly for me. Wolves and bears I can strangle, but I'm no match against those lowly earthworms. "Listen, little fellow," he said, "go in peace, I promise not to mess with you and your kind in the future, and if you have a wish, tell it to me, for I'd like to do you a favor."

"You've got long legs," said the drummer, "and can run faster than me. Carry me to Glass Mountain, and I'll send a signal to my troops to pull back, and they'll leave you in peace this once."

"Come here, worm," said the giant, "sit yourself on my shoulder, and I'll carry you wherever you wish."

The giant stood upright, and from his perch on the giant's shoulder the drummer drummed up a storm. The giant thought, That must be the signal for his troops to withdraw. After a while they met a second giant along the way, who took the drummer from the first giant and set him in his buttonhole. The drummer grabbed hold of the button that was as big as a key, held fast, and happily looked around. Then they came to a third giant, who plucked the drummer out of the buttonhole and plunked him on the rim of his hat. Up there the drummer went walking back and forth, and in the blue distance spotted a mountain over the treetops, and thought to himself, That must surely be Glass Mountain. Which it was indeed. The giant took another few steps, and they reached the foot of the mountain, where he dropped him off. The drummer insisted that he carry him all the way to the summit of Glass Mountain, but the giant shook his head, muttered something under his breath, and disappeared again in the forest.

Now the poor drummer stood in front of the mountain that was as high as three mountains stacked one on top of the other and as smooth as a mirror, and he had no idea how to get to the top. He started climbing, but to no avail – he always slipped back down again. If only I were a bird, he thought. But what good was it to wish it, he grew no wings. As he stood around at a loss for what to do, he spotted two men fighting not far away. He went toward them and saw that they were fighting over a saddle lying on the ground before them that each claimed as his own.

"What fools you are," he said. "You're fighting over a saddle and have no horse to ride."

"The saddle is well worth fighting for," one of the two men replied. "Whosoever sits on it and wishes to go anywhere, be it to the end of the world, once he's spoken the wish, he's transported there lickety-split. The saddle belongs to both of us and it's my turn to ride it, but the other guy won't let me."

"I'll settle your dispute this instant," said the drummer, then walked a little distance and stuck a white stick into the earth. He came back and said, "Now run to the stick, and whoever gets there first, it's his turn to ride."

The two men dashed off, but no sooner had they run a few paces than the drummer swung himself into the saddle, wished himself to the top of Glass Mountain, and before he turned his hand around there he was. On top of the mountain there was a flat plateau, on it stood a stone house, in front of the house lay a big pond, and behind it a deep dark forest. There was neither man nor beast to be seen about, only the wind rustling in the trees and the clouds hanging low over his head. He went to the door and knocked. At the third knock the door was opened by an old woman with a brown face and red eyes. She wore glasses on the bridge of her long nose, and after giving him the once-over, asked what he wanted.

"Food and shelter for the night," replied the drummer.

"That you may have," said the old woman, "if in exchange you do three chores."

"Why not?" he said. "I'm not afraid of work, however hard it is."

The old woman let him in, and gave him something to eat and a bed to sleep in. In the morning, as soon as he woke up, she took a thimble from her bony finger, handed it to the drummer, and said, "Now get to work and drain the pond outside with this thimble – but you must be done with it before nightfall, and all of the fish in the water must be selected and placed side by side according to kind and size."

"That's an odd task," said the drummer, but he went to the pond and got to work. He drained all morning, but how far can you get with a thimble in a big body of water, even if you keep draining for a thousand years? Come midday, he thought, It's no use and all the same if I work or not. So he stopped and sat down.

A girl came out of the house, set before him a basket of food, and said, "You sit around with such a sad expression. What's troubling you?"

He looked at her and saw that she was very beautiful. "Oh," he said, "if I cannot complete the first task, how will I ever manage with the other two? I went in search of a princess who is supposed to be living here, but I didn't find her. I'd best be shoving off."

"Stay here," said the girl. "I will help you in your trouble. You look tired, lay your head on my lap and sleep. When you awaken the task will be done."

The drummer didn't need to be told a second time. As soon as he shut his eyes, she turned a wishing ring on her finger and said, "Water up, fish out."

Whereupon, like a white fog, all the water rose out of the pond and wafted away with the other clouds, and the fish flipped about and leapt onto the shore and lay themselves neatly side by side, according to kind and size.

When the drummer woke up, he was stunned to see that the task had been accomplished.

The girl said, "One of the fishes isn't lying beside its sort but is all alone. When the old woman comes this evening and sees that all was done as she instructed, she will ask you, 'What is that fish doing there all alone?' Then fling the fish in her face and say, 'That one's for you, old witch!' "

That evening the old woman came by, and when she asked him the question, he flung the fish in her face. But she pretended not to take any notice, said nothing, and just scowled.

The next morning she said, "Yesterday you had it easy. I'll have to think up a more difficult task. Today you have to cut down the entire forest, cut the wood into planks, pile the planks in cords, and everything must be done by nightfall." She gave him an ax, a mallet, and two wedges. But the ax was made of lead, and the mallet and wedges of tin. As soon as he swung the ax, it twisted out of shape, and the mallet and wedges folded in two.

He did not know what to do, but at midday the girl came again to bring him food and comforted him. "Lay your head on my lap and sleep," she said. "When you wake up the task will accomplished."

She turned the wishing ring, and then and there the entire forest collapsed with a crash, and the wood split into planks and stacked itself into cords. It was as if an invisible giant had done the job.

When he woke up, the girl said, "You see, the wood is all split and stacked; just one limb is left over. When the old woman comes by this evening and asks about that limb, pick it up, strike her with it, and say, 'That's for you, old witch.' "

The old woman came. "You see," she said, "how easy it was, but why is that leftover limb lying about?"

"For you, old witch," he replied, and struck her with it.

But she pretended not to feel the blow, sneered, and said, "Tomorrow you will lay all that wood in a big pile and set it afire."

At daybreak he got up and started dragging the wood, but how can one man drag an entire forest? The work did not progress. But the girl did not leave him in the lurch. At midday she brought him his meal, and once he'd eaten, he lay his head in her lap and fell asleep. When he woke up, raging flames rose from the entire pile, the tongues of which reached the sky.

"Listen well," said the girl. "When the witch comes, she will assign you all kinds of tasks – do everything she asks without showing any fear, and she won't be able to do you any harm, but if she sees that you're frightened, the flames will lap you up and burn you to a crisp. Finally, once you've done everything she's asked, then grab her with your two hands and fling her into the glowing embers."

The girl went away and the old woman came skulking by. "Brrr! I'm freezing," she said. "Here is a fire to warm my old bones, now that feels good. But there's a block of wood that doesn't want to burn, go fetch it for me. If you do that last thing for me, you're free to go wherever you wish. So hop to it."

The drummer didn't hesitate for long and leapt into the flames, but they did him no harm, and not a hair on his head was singed. He hauled out the block and lay it on the ground. But no sooner did the wood touch the earth than it transformed itself, and the beautiful girl who had helped him out of his tough fixes was standing there before him – and by the silken, gold-embroidered clothes she wore he recognized that she was indeed the princess. But the old woman gave a nasty cackle and said, "You think you've got her, but you haven't got her yet." At that very moment she reached for the girl to drag her off, but he grabbed the old woman with both his hands, lifted her in the air, and swung her into the tongues of fire that lapped her up as though well-pleased to consume a witch.

Whereupon the princess looked at the drummer, and when she saw that he was a handsome youth, and considered that he had risked his life to save her, she reached out her hand to him and said, "You risked everything for me, but I will also do everything for you. If you promise to be true, then you will be my husband. We've riches enough, there's plenty of booty here that the witch amassed." She led him into the house, and there stood chests and chests full of treasure. They left the gold and silver and only took the diamonds. They did not want to stay any longer on Glass Mountain. Then he said to her, "Sit yourself beside me on this saddle, and we'll fly off like a bird."

"I don't like that old saddle," she said. "All I have to do is turn my wishing ring and we'll be home."

"Very well then," replied the drummer, "then wish us in front of the city gate."

In an instant they were there. The drummer said, "I want to go to my parents to let them know I'm okay. Wait for me here in the field, I'll be back soon."

"Oh," said the princess, "I beg you, be careful, don't kiss your parents on the right cheek when you see them, or else you'll forget everything, and I'll be left all alone, abandoned out here in the field."

"How could I forget you?" he said, and squeezed her hand, promising to be back very soon.

But when he entered his father's house, nobody knew who he was, so much had he changed, for the three days he spent on Glass Mountain were, in fact, three long years. Then he said who he was, and his parents wept for joy, wrapping their arms around his neck, and he was so moved in his heart that, forgetting the girl's words of warning, he kissed them on both cheeks. But as soon as he kissed them on the right cheek, he completely forgot the princess. He emptied his pockets and lay handfuls of the biggest diamonds on the table. His parents had no idea what to do with all those riches. The father built a splendid castle ringed by gardens, forests, and fields, as though a lord lived within. And when he was done, the mother said, "I have a girl for you. In three days' time the wedding will take place." The son acceded gladly to his parents' wishes.

The poor princess stood outside the gates of the city, waiting a long time for the youth's return. As darkness fell she said to herself, "He must surely have kissed his parents on the right cheek and forgotten me." Her heart was heavy with sadness, and she resolved to retreat to a lonesome cottage in the woods and never return to her father's court. Every evening she entered the city and walked past the drummer's house. He sometimes caught sight of her but did not recognize her. Then one day she heard people say, "Tomorrow he will be married."

Whereupon she said to herself, "Let me try to win back his heart."

Come the first day of the wedding celebration, she turned her ring and said, "Make me a dress as dazzling as the sun." No sooner were the words spoken than there before her lay a dress as glimmering as if it were woven of nothing but sunrays. When all the guests had gathered, she entered the hall. Everyone wondered at the lovely dress, most of all, the bride, and since she had a passion for beautiful garments, she went over to the stranger and asked if she would sell it to her. "Not for money," the stranger replied, "but if I may spend the first night outside the door of the bridegroom's room, I'll give it to you."

The bride could not quell her longing and agreed, but she mixed a sleeping potion in with the bridegroom's nightly glass of wine, which made him fall into a deep sleep. When everything was still, the princess huddled before his bedroom door, opened it a crack, and called out:

"Drummer, drummer, listen up.

Tell me, how could you clean forget

The girl who by your side on Glass Mountain sat?

Did I not trick the witch and save your life?

Did you not swear to make me your wife?

Drummer, drummer, listen up."

But it was no use, the drummer did not awaken, and come morning the princess had to leave without having gotten through to him.

On the evening of the second day of the wedding celebration, she turned her wishing ring and said, "Make me a dress as silvery as the moon." When she appeared at the festivities wearing the dress, she once again aroused the bride's longing and gave her the gown under the stipulation that she yet again be permitted to spend the night outside the bridegroom's bedroom door. And she called out in the still of the night:

"Drummer, drummer, listen up.

Tell me, how could you clean forget

The girl who by your side on Glass Mountain sat?

Did I not trick the witch and save your life?

Did you not swear to make me your wife?

Drummer, drummer, listen up."

But drugged by the sleeping potion, the drummer did not wake up. In the morning the princess sadly returned to her lonesome cottage in the woods. But the people in the house in which the drummer slept had heard the sad song of the strange girl and told the bridegroom about it. They also told him that he could not hear it because the bride had mixed a sleeping potion with his wine.

On the third night of the nuptial celebration the princess turned her wishing ring and said, "Make me a dress that glitters like the stars." When she appeared so attired at the party the bride was beside herself with longing to possess the dress that outshone all the others and said, "I must absolutely have it." The girl gave it to her, as she'd given the other two, in exchange for permission to spend the night outside the bridegroom's door. But this time the bridegroom did not drink his wine, but poured it out behind the bed. And as soon as all was still in the house, he heard a soft voice calling to him:

"Drummer, drummer, listen up.

Tell me, how could you clean forget

The girl who by your side on Glass Mountain sat?

Did I not trick the witch and save your life?

Did you not swear to make me your wife?

Drummer, drummer, listen up."

All of a sudden he remembered. "Dear God," he cried, "how could I callously betray her trust? It was the kiss I gave my parents on the right cheek with all the joy of my heart that made me forget." He leapt up, took the princess by the hand, and led her to his parents' bed. "This is my true bride," he said. "If I wed the other, I will do her a great injustice."

Once they heard the story of everything that had happened, the parents approved. The hall was once again lit up, drummers and trumpeters were fetched for the festivities, friends and family were invited to return, and the true wedding was celebrated in great happiness. The first bride kept the lovely dresses as compensation and declared herself well-pleased.

THE MARVELOUS MINSTREL

. .
.

There once was a marvelous minstrel who wandered through a forest, feeling so utterly lonesome, trying to distract himself thinking about this and that, and when he'd had it with his thoughts, he said to himself, "Time is dragging on so long in these woods. I think I'll fiddle forth a pleasant companion." So he took the fiddle from his back and fiddled a tune that resounded in the treetops. It wasn't long before a wolf came trotting forth out of the thicket. "Heavens!" said the minstrel. "A wolf I can do without."

But the wolf came closer and said to him, "My dear minstrel, what an enchanting tune you're fiddling! I'd like to learn it too."

"Easy does it," replied the minstrel. "Just do everything I tell you to do."

"Oh, minstrel," said the wolf, "I will obey you like a pupil his master."

The minstrel bid him to come along, and once they had walked a ways together, they came to an old oak tree whose trunk was hollow and split open down the middle. "See here," said the minstrel, "if you want to learn to fiddle, put your front paws in that slit." The wolf obeyed, but the minstrel hastened to pick up a stone, and with one blow wedged his paws in so tightly that the wolf was trapped like a prisoner. "Just wait here until I come back," said the minstrel and continued on his way.

A little while later he once again said to himself, "Time is dragging on so long in these woods. I think I'll fiddle forth another companion." So he took his fiddle from his back, and once again filled the wooded silence with a song. It wasn't long before a fox came creeping forth through the trees. "Heavens!" said the minstrel. "A fox is not my idea of a friend."

But the fox came furtively slinking over. "My dear minstrel, what an enchanting tune you're fiddling! I'd like to learn it too."

"Easy does it," said the minstrel. "Just do everything I tell you to do."

"Oh, minstrel," said the fox, "I will obey you like a pupil his master."

"Follow me," said the minstrel, and once they'd walked for a while they came to a footpath hemmed in on both sides by tall hedges. The minstrel halted, reached out and bent a little hazelnut tree to the ground, and held it down with his feet, then on the other side did the same with another spry sapling, and said, "Very well, little fox, if you want to learn something then stretch out your left front paw." The fox obeyed, and the minstrel bound his paw to the tree on his left. "Now the right one," he said, which he proceeded to bind to the tree on his right. And once he'd checked that the knots were tied tightly enough, he let go with his feet, and the trees sprung back, hurling the little fox up in the air so that he dangled and flounced, suspended high above the ground.

"Just wait here till I come back," said the minstrel, and continued on his way.

And yet again he said to himself, "Time is dragging on so long in these woods. I think I'll fiddle forth another companion," and grabbed his fiddle and filled the wooded silence with a song. Whereupon a hare came leaping forth. "Heavens!" said the minstrel. "What am I to do with a hare?"

"My dear minstrel," said the little hare, "what an enchanting tune you're fiddling! I'd like to learn it too."

"Easy does it," said the minstrel. "Just do everything I tell you to do."

"Oh, minstrel," said the hare, "I will obey you like a pupil his master."

They went on for a while together until they came to a clearing in the woods where stood an aspen tree. The minstrel bound a long twine around the hare's neck, the other end of which he knotted to the tree. "Lively now, little hare, run twenty times around the tree," the minstrel commanded, and the hare obeyed, and once it had run twenty times around, the twine twisted twenty times around the tree, and the hare was caught fast, tug and tear as it might, the twine just dug into its soft neck.

"Just wait here till I come back," said the minstrel and continued on his way.

The wolf, meanwhile, squirmed and tugged and gnawed so long at the stone until it freed its paws and slipped them out of the split in the tree trunk. Huffing and puffing with fury, it ran after the minstrel and wanted to tear him to shreds. When the fox saw it running by, it started to whine and cried out at the top of its lungs, "Brother Wolf, help me please, the minstrel has deceived me." The wolf tugged down the little tree until the cord snapped in two and freed the fox, who went with the wolf to take revenge on the minstrel. They found the fastened hare, which they likewise released, whereupon they all went in search of their sworn enemy.

Yet again did the minstrel stroke his fiddle along the way, and this time he got lucky. The sweet strains struck the ear of a poor woodcutter, who, no sooner having heard it, whether he wanted to or not, felt compelled to stop working, and with the hatchet under his arm, came walking over, drawn by the music. "Finally I've found the right companion," said the minstrel, "for I wanted to bide my time with a human being, not a wild beast." And he started playing so splendidly and sweetly that the poor woodcutter just stood there, stunned, his heart bursting with joy. And as he stood like that, the wolf, the fox, and the hare came running up, and he sensed their evil intent. So he raised the flashing hatchet over his head and stood before the minstrel as if to say: Over my dead body. Whereupon the wild beasts took fright and hightailed it back into the woods. The minstrel played the man another tune to thank him and then continued on his way.

THE MUSICIANS OF BREMEN

. .
.

Aman had a donkey that had faithfully lugged heavy sacks of grain to the mill for many years, but the poor beast's strength had finally given out, so that he was no longer up to the task. The man thought of taking him to the horse skinner, but the donkey got wind of this, ran off, and set out for Bremen, where he thought he might make a go of it as a street musician. After walking for a while he came upon a hunting hound lying by the wayside, panting like someone who had run himself ragged.

"Why are you panting like that, Pooch?" asked the donkey.

"Oh," said the hound, "because I'm old and getting weaker day by day, and no longer fit for the hunt. My master wanted to do me in, so I took to my heels, but how am I to feed myself?"

"You know what," said the donkey, "I'm on my way to Bremen to become a street musician. Why don't you come along and join my band. I'll play the lute and you can beat a drum."

The hound was happy and they continued on their way. After a while they found a cat seated by the wayside that made a face as miserable as sin.

"What's eating you, old Puss?" asked the donkey.

"You want me to smile when I'm done for?" replied the cat. "Because I'm of an age when my teeth are dull and I'd rather sit curled up by the oven than chase after mice, my mistress wanted to drown me. I escaped in the nick of time, but what am I going to do now?"

"Come along with us to Bremen. You're good at howling at night, why not become a street musician?"

The cat agreed and came along. Whereupon the three fugitives came upon a farmyard in front of which sat a rooster crowing its lungs out.

"Why the bone-tingling lament?" asked the donkey. "What's the matter?"

"I have crowed faithfully and prophesied good weather," said the rooster, "for the day when our blessed Mother in heaven washed the shirt of the Christ Child and hung it out to dry. But because tomorrow is Sunday and guests are coming, the merciless lady of the house told the cook to make a soup of me, and tonight I'm to be beheaded. So I'm crowing my lungs out as long as I still can."

"Pipe down, you Cock-a-Doodle," said the donkey. "Better come with us. We're headed for Bremen, where you'll surely find a better fate than death. You've got a good voice, why not make music with us?"

The rooster agreed, and all four went on their way.

But Bremen was too far to reach in a day, and as darkness fell they came to a forest where they planned to spend the night. The donkey and the hound lay themselves down under a great tree, the cat and the rooster clambered up the branches, but the rooster flew all the way up to the topmost branch, where he felt the safest. Before falling asleep, he took another look around in the direction of all four winds. In the distance, the rooster thought he saw sparks flickering and called down to his comrades that there must be a house nearby, since he could see its glow.

So the donkey said, "Then we'd best rouse ourselves and hobble over. We can't catch any shut-eye here." The hound thought that a few bones with a little meat on them would do him good. So they made their way toward where the light shone, and soon saw it glowing ever more intensely, until they found themselves in front of a brightly lit den of thieves. Being the biggest, the donkey drew near and peaked in through the window.

"What do you see in there, Old Ned?" asked the rooster.

"What do I see?" replied the donkey. "There's a table set with plentiful food and drink and the thieves are sitting around stuffing their faces."

"That'd make a tasty tidbit," said the rooster.

"That it would, if only we could get to it!" the donkey agreed.

Then the animals put their heads together to try to figure out how to chase the thieves out, and finally they came up with a plan. The donkey had to lift one hoof onto the window ledge, the hound had to leap on the donkey's back, the cat had to climb on top of the hound, and finally, the rooster flew up and landed on the cat's head. As soon as they managed, at an agreed-upon signal they started making their music: the donkey hee-hawed, the hound barked, the cat meowed, and the rooster crowed; then they tumbled in through the window, so that the windowpanes rattled. The thieves leapt up at the terrible racket, convinced it must be a ghost, and flew in terror out into the forest. Whereupon the four friends sat themselves down at the table and feasted on the leftovers, eating like there was no tomorrow.

Once the musicians had eaten their fill, they put out the light and sought comfortable corners in which to rest their bones, each according to his kind and comfort. The donkey lay down in the rubbish heap outside, the hound behind the door, the cat on the hearth above the warm ashes, and the rooster sat on the ceiling beam – and because they were so weary from their long walk they soon fell fast asleep.

Once midnight had passed and the thieves saw that the lights no longer burned in the house and everything was quiet, the captain said, "We shouldn't have let ourselves scatter like chickens," and ordered a member of the band to go to the house to check things out. The scout found everything quiet, went into the kitchen to light a torch, and taking the glowing fiery eyes of the cat for live charcoal, he held out a stick to catch fire. But the cat had no fondness for fun and games, and leapt in his face, hissing and scratching. The thief took an awful fright and wanted to run out the back door, but the hound that lay there jumped up and bit him in the leg; and when he ran across the yard and passed the rubbish heap, the donkey gave him a mighty kick with its hind legs; and awakened by the ruckus, the rooster cried down from the roof: "Cock-a-doodle-do!"

The thief ran as fast as he could back to the captain and reported: "There's a gruesome witch seated inside the house, she hissed at me and scratched my face with her long fingernails; a man with a long knife is planted at the back door, he stabbed me in the leg; and in the yard lies a terrible monster that clubbed me with a cudgel; and up on the roof sits a judge who cried out, 'Bring me the knave!' So I ran for my life."

From then on the thieves no longer dared enter the house, but the four musicians of Bremen liked it so much they didn't want to leave. And the last one to tell me the story, his breath is still warm.

THE CHILDREN OF HAMELN

In *the year* 1284 a curious man appeared in Hameln. He wore a coat of many-colored cloth, which is why he was known as *Bundting*, Gaudy Guy. He said he was a ratcatcher and promised, for a considerable compensation, to rid the city of all mice and rats. The burghers of Hameln came to an agreement with him, assuring a certain sum of money. The ratcatcher pulled out a little pipe and blew on it, and then the rats and mice came running out of every house and gathered around him. And when he determined that there were none left, he headed out of the city and they all followed him, and he led them to the bank of the River Weser. There he undressed and walked into the water, whereupon all the rodents followed, and diving into the drink, promptly drowned.

But no sooner were the burghers delivered from the infestation than they thought twice about paying the promised price and, coming up with all kinds of excuses, refused to give the man what he asked. He stormed off angry and embittered.

At seven in the morning, others say at noon, on the twenty-sixth of June,

Saint John's and Saint Paul's Day, he reappeared, this time dressed as a hunter with a strange red hat, his face twisted into a terrible grimace, and once again let his pipe be heard in the streets of Hameln. Presently, instead of rats and mice, children in great numbers, boys and girls as young as four, came running, among them also the grown daughter of the Bürgermeister. They all followed him, and he led them into the cleft in a mountain, where they and he disappeared.

This was witnessed by a nursemaid with a child in her arm, who followed him from afar, turned around thereafter, and brought word of it back to the city. With heavy hearts, the distraught parents searched high and low for their lost children; the mothers let out a pitiful wailing and weeping. Messengers were immediately sent out to comb every body of water and square inch of land in the vicinity, inquiring if anyone had seen hide or hair of the children, but to no avail. In all, a hundred and thirty children were lost.

It is said by some that two who had lagged behind, returned; one of them was blind, the other deaf, so that the blind one could not show but only tell how they'd followed the piper; and the deaf one, on the other hand, indicated the place where the others disappeared but had not heard a sound. Others tell that a little lad who followed in his shirtsleeves turned back to fetch his coat, which is why he survived the misfortune, for once he returned, the others had already disappeared into the hole in a hill that is still shown to this day.

The street along which the children passed on their way out the gate was still, in the middle of the eighteenth century (as it is today), called the Street of Silence, since no dancing or music was permitted. Indeed, when a bride was serenaded on her way to church, the musicians had to stop playing on that street. The mountain near Hameln in which the children disappeared is called the Poppenberg, to the left and right of which two stone crosses were erected. Some say the children were led into a cave and came out again in Siebenbürgen.

The burghers of Hameln had the occurrence recorded in their civic register and made a custom of counting the years and days elapsed since the loss of their children. According to Seyfried, the twenty-second, rather than the twenty-sixth, of June is the recorded date. A plaque with the following lines hangs on the wall of the Rathaus:

In 1284, the year of our Lord
Hameln registered the sad record
Of a hundred and thirty children here born
By a piper nabbed and ever mourned.

And on the new gate of the city is inscribed:

Centrum ter denos cum magnus ab urbe puellos
Duxerat ante annos CCLXXII condita porta fuit.

In the year 1572 the Bürgermeister had the story depicted in the pane of a stained-glass window along with the accompanying caption, which is unreadable today. A medallion marking the event is also affixed.

THE MASTER THIEF

O*ne day* an old man sat with his wife in front of a humble house to take a short rest from his work. Then a splendid carriage drawn by four horses came rolling up, and out stepped a well-dressed gentleman. The weary peasant got up, went over to the gentleman, and asked him what he wanted and how he could be of service. The stranger reached out his hand to the old man and said, "I have no other wish but to enjoy a rustic dish. Fix me up a plate of potatoes the way you like them, and I'll sit myself down at your table and devour them with pleasure."

The peasant smiled and said, "You must be a count or a prince, or perhaps a duke, fancy folk sometimes have such whims. We'll see what we can do." His wife went to the kitchen and started washing and grating potatoes, intending to prepare a plate of dumplings, peasant style. While she was busy whipping them up, the peasant said to the stranger, "Come with me, in the meantime, to my vegetable garden. I still have a few chores to attend to." He had dug holes in the ground and wanted to plant trees.

"Have you no children who could help you with your work?" the stranger asked.

"No," replied the peasant. "I did indeed have a son," he added, "but it's been years since he went off into the world. He was a wayward lad, crafty and sly, but he didn't want to learn anything and kept on playing tricks. Finally he ran away, and I never heard from him again."

The old man took a sapling, set it in the hole, and planted a pole beside it, and once he'd shoveled the earth back in around it and stamped it down with his feet, he bound the sapling below, above, and in the middle to the pole with a straw cord.

"But tell me," said the gentleman, "why don't you tie up that knotty twisted tree over there in the corner that's almost bent down to the ground, so that it may grow straight?"

The old man smiled and said, "Sir, you speak like you know what you're talking about, but I can tell you haven't spent much time gardening. That tree over there is old and twisted, nobody can make it grow straight again. Trees can only be trained when they're young."

"It's just like your son," said the stranger. "If you'd brought him up right when he was still young, he wouldn't have run away. He too must have grown hard and knotty by now."

"No doubt," replied the old man. "It's been a long time since he went away. He must have changed considerably."

"Would you still recognize him if he were standing here before you?" asked the stranger.

"Probably not by his face," replied the peasant, "but he had a birthmark on his shoulder the size of a bean."

As soon as the peasant said this, the stranger took his coat off, bared his shoulder, and showed him the bean-shaped birthmark.

"God in heaven," cried the old man, "you are indeed my son," and the love he felt for his own flesh and blood welled up in his heart. "But how can you be my son?" he added. "You've become a fine gentleman and live in the lap of luxury. How did you get rich?"

"Oh, Father," replied the son, "this tree was bound to no pole, he didn't grow up straight – and now he's too old and it's too late to straighten him out. How did I get rich, you ask. I became a thief. But don't worry, I'm a master thief. There's no lock I can't pick or bolt I can't break, whatever I want is mine. I don't steal like a common thief, I only take from the surplus of the rich. Poor people have nothing to fear from me. I'd rather give to than take from them. And I won't waste my time with a heist that doesn't demand the utmost effort, stealth, and finesse to bring off."

"Oh, my son," said the father, "a thief is still a thief. It won't end well, I tell you."

The father took him to his mother, and when she heard it was her son, she wept for joy, but when he told her he'd become a master thief, a second stream of tears ran down her face. Finally she said, "Thief or no thief, you are still my son, and my eyes are glad to see you again."

They sat down at the table, and he ate again with his parents the poor man's dish he hadn't tasted in years.

The father said, "If the lord, the count in the castle over there, discovers who you are and what you do, he won't take you in his arms and rock you as he did at your baptism when you were born. He'll let you swing from the gallows."

"Don't fret, dear Father, I know my craft, he won't do a thing to me. I'll go present myself to him today." When night fell, the master thief set out in his carriage to the castle.

The count received him with the utmost courtesy, as he took him for a gentleman of quality. But when the stranger revealed who he was, the count turned pale and went silent for a while. Finally he said to him, "You are my godchild, so I will have mercy on you. Since you claim to be a master thief, I'll put your skill to the test, but if you fail, you'll dangle with the hangman's daughter, and the crowing of ravens will be your wedding music."

"Sir count," replied the master thief, "think up three tests as hard as they might be, and if I don't succeed you can do with me as you wish."

The count pondered for a while, and then he said, "Very well then, first off, you will steal my horse from the stable; second, you will steal the sheets out from under my wife and myself as we sleep, and my wife's wedding ring to boot, without waking us; third and last, you will steal the pastor and the sexton out of the church. Mind all I said, or it'll cost you your neck."

The master thief proceeded to the nearest city. There he bought the clothes off the back of an old peasant woman and put them on. Then he applied brown makeup to his face and painted in wrinkles, so that no one would recognize him. Finally he filled a jug with old Hungarian wine in which he mixed a strong sleep potion. He placed the jug in a basket hung from his back and made his way with deliberately tottering steps to the count's castle. It was already dark by the time he arrived. There he sat himself down on a flat stone in the courtyard and began to cough like an old woman suffering from consumption and rubbed his hands together as though he trembled with cold. Soldiers sat around a fire in front of the stable. One of them noticed the old woman and called to her, "Come join us, old mother, and warm yourself by our fire. You've got no place to rest your weary bones. Better take what you can get." The old woman stumbled over, took the basket from her shoulders, and sat down beside the fire.

"What do you have there in that jug, old biddy?" a soldier asked.

"A swallow of wine," she replied. "I peddle it to the thirsty. For a coin or two and a few kind words I'll gladly give you a glassful."

"Here, give us a gulp," said the soldier, and once he'd downed a glass, he winked and said, "It's a good vintage, old mother, I'll gladly have another glass." Whereupon he emptied another glass, and the others promptly followed his example. "Hey, fellas," the drunken soldier cried to the stableboys, "there's an old lady here peddling wine that's as old as she is. Come have a drop. It'll warm you better than this fire."

The old woman carried the jug into the stable. One of the stable hands was seated on the count's saddled steed, another held the bridle in his hand, a third held it by the tail. She poured as much as they wanted until the jug was empty. In a little while the bridle fell out of the one stableboy's hand, and he leaned back and began snoring. The other one let go of the tail, lay back, and snored even louder. The one in the saddle stayed seated where he was, but leaned forward against the horse's mane, fell asleep, and snorted like a smithy. The soldiers outside had long since fallen asleep and lay around on the ground without moving, as if they were made of stone. As soon as the master thief assured himself that his scheme had worked, he gave the stableboy holding the bridle a rope to hold, and the one holding the tail a straw switch. But what was he to do with the one who sat asleep in the saddle? He didn't want to shove him out of the saddle, lest he awaken and cry out to the others. But he had an idea. He unfastened the saddle cinch, attached it to a few cords that hung from metal rings embedded in the wall, raised saddle and rider in midair, and tied the loose ends of the cords tightly to the doorpost. It was easy enough to untie the horse from the chain, but had he ridden it across the flagstones of the courtyard the clip-clop of its hooves would have been heard in the castle. So first he bound rags around each of its hooves, and then carefully led it out, swung himself into the saddle, and made off with it.

At the break of day, the master thief swung himself again into the saddle of the stolen horse and rode it to the castle. The count had just awakened and looked out the window. "Good morning, sir count," the master thief called up to him. "Here is the horse that I successfully stole out of your stable, and if you care to have a look in the stable you'll see how comfortable your guards have made themselves."

The count had to laugh, then he said, "This once you succeeded, but the second task won't be so easy. And I warn you, if next we cross paths as thief and target, then I will treat you as a thief."

That evening when the countess went to bed she balled up the fingers of her left hand around the wedding ring, and the count said, "All the doors are locked and bolted, and I'll stay awake and lie in wait for the thief. If he climbs in through the window, I'll shoot him down."

But when it got dark, the master thief hastened to the gallows, cut down a poor sinner he found swinging there, and carried him on his back to the castle. There he leaned a ladder against the castle wall, hoisted the dead man onto his shoulders, and started climbing up. Once he had climbed high enough so that the head of the dead man appeared in the window, the count, who lay awake in bed, pressed the trigger of his pistol. Whereupon the master thief let the poor sinner fall to the ground, leapt off the ladder, and hid in a corner.

The night was so brightly lit by the moon that the master thief could clearly make out the count as he climbed down the ladder and carried the dead man into the garden. There he began digging a hole in which to bury him. Now, thought the thief, is the right time, and he nimbly slipped out of hiding and climbed the ladder up into the countess's bedroom. "Dear wife," he said, mimicking the voice of the count, "the thief is dead, but he was after all my godchild and more of a prankster than a villain – I won't want to put him to public shame, and I feel bad for his poor parents. Before daybreak I myself will bury him in the garden, so that no one gets wind of the matter. Give me a bedsheet, and I'll wrap the corpse in it and dig him under like a dog." The countess gave him the bedsheet. "You know what," the thief went on, "I'm feeling generous, give me the ring. The poor unfortunate risked his life to get it, so let him take it with him to the grave." Under the circumstances, the countess did not want to have words with her husband, and with a heavy heart she pulled the ring from her finger and handed it to him. The thief made off with both bits of booty and safely reached his hideout before the count had finished patting down the grave in the garden.

What a face the count made when the following morning the master thief appeared with bedsheet and ring in hand! "Are you a sorcerer?" he said to him. "Who dug you out of the grave in which I myself laid you and brought you back to life?"

"You did not bury me," said the thief, "but rather that poor sinner who dangled from the gallows." Whereupon he detailed just how he'd done it. And the count had to admit that he was indeed a cunning and canny thief.

"But you're not done yet," he added, "you still have a third task to accomplish, and if you don't succeed, God help you." In response to which the master thief just smiled and made no reply.

At nightfall he came to the village church with a long sack on his back, a bundle under his arm, and a lantern in hand. The sack was filled with crabs, and in the bundle he had short wax candles. He sat himself down in the graveyard, pulled a crab out of the sack, and stuck a candle on its back; then he lit the candle, lowered the crab to the ground, and let it run free. He fetched another out of the sack and did the same with it, and again with another crab, until the sack was empty. Whereupon he put on a long black gown that looked like a monk's habit and glued a gray beard to his chin. When at last he was completely unrecognizable, he took the sack in which he'd carried the crabs, entered the church, and climbed the pulpit.

The bells just struck twelve, and when the last knell went silent he cried out in a shrill voice, "Hear ye, all sinners, the end has come, Judgment Day has come – hear ye, hear ye! Whoever wants to go to heaven, let him crawl into this sack. I am Saint Peter, who opens and shuts the gates of heaven. Look there, the dead are wandering in the graveyard and gathering up their bones. Come one, come all, and crawl into my sack, the world has come to an end."

His cry echoed throughout the village. The pastor and the sexton lived nearest the church and were the first to hear it, and when they spotted the lights ambling around the graveyard, they immediately fathomed that something was amiss and hastened to the church. They listened for a while to the sermon, then the sexton nudged the pastor and said, "It might not be a bad idea if before the break of Judgment Day the two of us found an easy access to heaven."

"My sentiments precisely," replied the pastor. "If you're willing, let's get going."

"That I am," replied the sexton. "You first, pastor. I'll follow."

So the pastor went first and climbed the steps to the pulpit, where the master thief opened his sack. The pastor crawled in, and the sexton followed. The thief promptly fastened the sack tightly, grabbed it, and dragged it down the pulpit steps – whenever the heads of the two arrant fools struck against the steps, the thief cried out, "We're climbing the mountain." Then he dragged them in a similar manner through the village, and when they came to puddles, he cried out, "Now we're climbing through the rain-soaked clouds." And when at last he dragged them up the castle steps, he cried, "Now we're climbing the steps to heaven and will soon be there." And when they reached the head of the stairs he shoved the sack into the dovecote, and when the doves flapped and fluttered about, he said, "The angels are so happy they're flapping their wings." Then he shut the dovecote latch and went away.

The next morning he appeared before the count and told him that he had accomplished the third task, and stolen the pastor and sexton out of the church.

"Where did you leave them?" asked the count.

"They're lying bundled in a sack in the dovecote and think they're in heaven."

The count climbed up to the dovecote to see for himself if the thief was telling the truth. When he released the pastor and the sexton from their keep, he said, "You are indeed an ace of thieves and have won your wager. This once I'll allow you to escape with your head, but you better make haste and leave my land, for if ever I see hide or hair of you again hereabouts, you can count on the gallows."

The master thief bid his parents farewell, left home once more, and no one ever heard from him again.

THE BLUE LIGHT

There once was a soldier who had faithfully served his king for many years. But when the war was over, the king said to the soldier, who had suffered many wounds and so was no longer fit for combat, "You can go home now, I won't be needing your services – but don't expect any more money from me. I only pay those who can earn their keep."

Now the soldier, who had no idea how to make ends meet, went off with a heavy heart and walked all day until evening when he came to a forest. When darkness fell, he saw a light, and approaching it, he came to a house in which lived a witch. "Give me shelter for the night, a bite to eat, and a drop to drink," he said to her, "or else I'm done for."

"Oho!" she replied. "Who would dare aid a deserted soldier? But I will show you mercy and take you in if you do what I ask."

"What do you want me to do?" asked the soldier.

"I want you to plow my garden tomorrow."

The soldier consented, and the next day he worked until he dropped, but come evening he hadn't finished the job.

"It's clear," said the witch, "that you can't do any more today. I'll keep you another night, in exchange for which I want you to chop me a cartload of firewood tomorrow."

The soldier took the whole of the next day to get the job done, and come evening, the witch offered to put him up for another night. "Tomorrow," she said, "I only ask that you do me a small service. Behind my house there is an old well that has run dry. My light fell in, and it burns blue and never goes out. You must fetch it for me."

The next day the old hag led him to the well and lowered him down in a basket. He found the blue light and made a sign for her to hoist him back up, which she proceeded to do. But when he got close to the rim, she reached out her hand and wanted to grab the light.

"Not so fast," he said, sensing her evil intent. "I'll only give you the light once I have both my feet firmly planted on dry ground." Whereupon the witch flew into a rage, let him drop back down into the well, and walked away.

The poor soldier fell to the damp bottom without a bruise, and the blue light kept burning, but what good did that do him? Facing his inevitable death, he sat around sadly for a while, when he happened to reach into his pocket and found his pipe half stuffed with tobacco. This will be my last pleasure, he thought, and pulled out the pipe, lit it on the blue light, and started smoking. As the cloud of smoke rose around him, all at once a little black man appeared before him and asked, "Master, what is your wish?"

"How can a lowly creature like me command anything of you?" the flabbergasted soldier replied.

"I must do," said the little man, "whatever you ask."

"Good," said the soldier. "So first help me get out of this well."

The little man took him by the hand and led him through underground passageways, the soldier remembering to take along the blue light. Along the way the little man showed him the treasures the witch had amassed and hidden there, and the soldier took as much gold as he could carry. Once they reached the surface, he said to the little man, "Now go and tie up the old witch and take her to prison." A little while later she went riding by with a terrible shriek, quick as the wind, on the back of a wild tomcat. And shortly thereafter the little man returned. "Everything's arranged," he said, "and the witch is already dangling from the gallows. Master," the little man continued, "what is your next wish?"

"Nothing at the moment," the solider replied, "you can go home, just be sure to come when I call."

"That won't be necessary," said the little man. "All you have to do is kindle your pipe with the blue light, and I'll be standing there before you." With these words he disappeared.

The soldier returned to the city he came from. He went to the finest inn and had a fine suit of clothes made, then asked the innkeeper to furnish a room for him as lavishly as possible. Once it was done and the soldier moved in, he called the little black man and said, "I faithfully served the king, but he sent me packing and would have let me starve to death. Now it's my turn to take revenge."

"What should I do?" asked the little man.

"Late at night when the king's daughter is in bed, bring her here fast asleep. She will serve as my chambermaid."

The little man said, "That's easy enough for me, but for you it'll be a bit of risky business. When the king finds out, you'll be in big trouble."

At the stroke of twelve, the door flew open, and the little man carried the king's daughter in.

"Aha, is that you?" the soldier cried. "Get to work now! Go fetch a broom and sweep my room." When she was done, he had her approach his chair, then he stretched his feet out and said, "Pull my boots off," which she did, whereupon he flung them in her face, and she had to pick them up, and clean and polish them until they sparkled. But she obeyed his every command in silence and with half-closed eyes. At the cock's first crow the little man returned with her to the royal castle and lay her back in bed.

That morning, when she got up, she went to her father and told him she'd had a strange dream. "I was carried through the streets at lightning speed and brought to a soldier's room, whom I had to serve hand and foot as a chamber-maid, and do all the menial tasks, sweep up and polish his boots. It was just a dream, yet I'm so tired as if I'd really done it."

"The dream might not have been an illusion," said the king. "I'll give you a bit of advice – stuff your pockets full of peas and tear a tiny hole in your pocket. Should you be picked up again, the peas will fall out and leave a trail on the street."

Standing by, invisible, the little man listened in and heard everything the king said. That night, as he once again carried the sleeping princess through the streets, peas did indeed fall out of her pocket but they left no trace, since the crafty little man had previously strewn peas in every street. Again the princess had to serve the soldier hand and foot until the cock's first crow.

The following morning the king sent his servants out to follow the trail, but their effort was to no avail, since children sat on every street picking up peas. "Last night it rained peas," they said, laughing.

"We have to think up something else," said the king. "Keep your shoes on when you go to bed, and before you come back from wherever they take you, hide a shoe. I'll find the culprit all right."

Again the little black man overheard the king's ruse, and when the soldier ordered him that night to once again carry off the princess, he counseled him against it, saying, "Against such stealth there's nothing I can do. If they find the shoe at your place, things may go badly for you."

"Do as I say," replied the soldier, and for the third straight night the princess had to serve him hand and foot. But she hid a shoe under the bed when the little man carried her back.

The next morning the king had the entire city searched for his daughter's shoe, and it was found at the soldier's lodgings. Heeding the little man's advice, the soldier had taken flight, but he was soon captured and thrown into jail. In his hasty departure, the soldier had left behind his most precious possessions, the blue light and the gold, and had only a ducat left in his pocket. Standing in chains at the window of his prison cell, he saw an old comrade strolling by. The soldier rapped on the window bars, and when his comrade came over, he said to him, "Please be so kind as to fetch me the little bundle I left back at the inn. I'll give you a ducat if you do." The comrade ran to the soldier's old digs and brought him what he asked for. As soon as the prisoner was alone again, he lit his pipe and called forth the little man.

"Fear not," the little man said to his master. "Go where they take you, and let them do what they will, just don't forget the blue light."

The next day the soldier was brought to trial, and although he hadn't done anything evil, the judge condemned him to death. As he was led off to the gallows, he begged the king for one last kindness.

"What is it?" asked the king.

"That I may be permitted to smoke my pipe on the way to my execution."

"You can smoke three, for all I care," replied the king, "but don't think I'll grant you your life."

Whereupon the soldier pulled out his pipe and lit it with the blue light, and as soon as a few smoke rings rose above him, the little man appeared before him with a little club in his hand, and said, "What does my master wish?"

"Go strike down the false judge and his henchmen, and don't spare the king who treated me so badly."

Then quick as lightning, the little man leapt forward and, slam-bam, went to work, and whomever he struck with the club fell down and never rose again. The king took fright and begged for his life, in exchange for which he gave the soldier his kingdom and his daughter for a wife.

TOM THUMB

There once was a poor plowman who sat in the evening by the hearth and stoked the fire, and his wife sat and spun. "It's so sad that we have no children," he said. "Our house is so quiet, and all the other houses around us are loud and gay."

"Yes," said his wife with a sigh, "if only we had but one child, and even if he were the size of a thumb I'd be happy. We'd love him with all our heart."

It so happened that the woman fell ill and seven months later she gave birth to a child who was well proportioned in every way, but no taller than a thumb. Whereupon the couple remarked, "He's just as we wished, and he will be our darling boy," and because of his size they called him Tom Thumb. Every day they fed him his fill, yet the child grew no taller but stayed as small as he was at that first hour. Still he had a savvy look in his eyes and soon proved to be a quick-witted and nimble little fellow who succeeded at every task he undertook.

One day the plowman prepared to go into the woods to chop wood, and he muttered to himself, "If only I had someone to bring the cart to fetch the wood for me."

"Oh, Father," cried Tom Thumb, "I'll bring the cart, you can count on that. It will be waiting for you in the woods when you're done."

The man laughed and said, "How in heaven's name do you propose to do it? You're too small to lead the horse by the leash."

"Never mind, Father, if Mother will harness the horse I'll sit myself in his ear and call out the right directions."

"Very well," said the father, "we'll give it a try."

At the appointed hour, his mother harnessed the horse and sat Tom Thumb in the horse's ear, whereupon the little one called out directions: "Giddyap! On the double!" The horse advanced as if led by a master carter, and the cart rolled in the right direction toward the woods. Now it so happened that just as they rounded a bend and the little one cried out "Hut! Hut!," two men approached.

"Well for crying out loud," said the one, "will you get a load of that? There's a cart rolling along, and the carter's calling out to the horse, but he's nowhere in sight."

"There's something funny going on here," said the other. "Let's follow the cart and see where it leads."

But the cart rolled right into the woods and straight to the place where the felled wood lay. No sooner did Tom Thumb see his father than he called out to him, "See, Father, here I am with the cart. Now take me down."

The father took hold of the horse with his left hand and with his right pulled his little son out of the horse's ear and put him down on a stalk of straw, where he sat cheerfully.

When the two strangers set eyes on Tom Thumb, they were struck dumb with amazement. Then the one said to the other, "Hey, that little fellow could make our fortune if we took him to a big city and had people pay for a peek – we'll buy him." So they approached the plowman and said, "Sell us the little man. He'll have it good with us."

"No," said the father, "he's my dear heart and I wouldn't sell him for all the money in the world."

But upon hearing the proposition, Tom Thumb climbed the folds of his father's coat, hoisted himself up to his shoulder, and whispered in his ear, "Father, go ahead and sell me. I'll be back in no time."

So the father sold him to the two men for a handsome sum.

"Where do you want to sit?" they said to him.

"Oh, just set me on the rim of your hat so I can go walking around and get the lay of the land without falling off. They did as he wished, and as soon as Tom Thumb took leave of his father they set out on their way. They kept on walking until dusk, then the little one spoke up: "Let me down a moment, nature calls."

"Just stay up there," replied the man on whose head he sat. "Don't worry about it, the birds also sometimes let drop on my hat."

"No," said Tom Thumb, "good manners matter to me – hurry up and let me down."

The man took his hat off and set the little fellow on the ground, whereupon he jumped off and crept among the clumps of earth, then suddenly slipped into a mouse hole he'd been looking for. "Good evening, kind sirs, be on your way without me!" he cried out and laughed. They came running over and poked around the mouse hole with their walking sticks, but it was no use. Tom Thumb crawled ever deeper in, and since it was soon pitch-black out they were obliged to return home, grumbling and with an empty purse.

When Tom Thumb saw that they were gone, he crawled back out of that handy little grotto. "It's so dangerous fumbling around a farm field in the dark," said he. "A body might easily break a leg or worse!" Fortunately he happened upon an empty snail shell. "Thank God," said he, "it's just the place to find shelter for the night," and promptly slipped in.

Not long thereafter, when he was just about to fall asleep, he heard two men passing overhead, one of whom said to the other, "How shall we go about relieving the rich pastor of his silver and gold?"

"It's as easy as pie!" cried out Tom Thumb.

"What was that?" The one thief took fright. "I heard someone say something."

They stopped dead in their tracks and listened. Then Tom Thumb spoke up again: "Take me along, and I'll help you."

"Where are you hiding?"

"Just search on the ground and take heed of where the voice is coming from," he replied.

The thieves finally found him and lifted him up in the air. "You little twerp, what good would you do us?"

"Easy does it," he replied. "I'll crawl through the iron bars into the pastor's room and hand you everything you like."

"Very well," they said, "let's see what you can do."

When they reached the rectory, Tom Thumb crept into the pastor's room and promptly cried out at the top of his lungs, "Do you want everything?"

The thieves took fright and said, "Speak in a whisper, so you don't wake everyone up."

But Tom Thumb pretended not to understand, and cried out again, "What do you want? Do you want everything?"

Which roused the cook who, sleeping in the room next door, sat up in bed and cocked an ear.

In their terror the thieves had run back a bit, but finally they pulled themselves together and thought, The little fellow is kidding us. They came back and whispered to him, "Up and at 'em now. Pass something to us."

Whereupon Tom Thumb cried out again at the top of his lungs, "I'll give you everything, just reach your hands in for it!"

The maid heard these words clearly, leapt out of bed, and stumbled to the door. The thieves ran for their lives, as though a wild dog were on their trail, but noticing nothing, the maid went to light a lantern. When she approached, Tom Thumb slipped out to the barn without being seen. After inspecting every corner and finding nothing, the maid finally returned to bed and thought she must have been dreaming with open eyes and ears.

Tom Thumb climbed around in the hay and found himself a cozy place to curl up and sleep – he intended to rest until daybreak and then make his way home to his parents. But other experiences lay in store for him. Life is full of trials and tribulations! At the crack of dawn the maid climbed out of bed to feed the livestock. Her first task was to go to the barn to grab an armful of hay, precisely that armful, alas, in which Tom Thumb lay asleep. But he slept so soundly that he was oblivious and did not blink an eye until he found himself in the mouth of a cow that had snatched him up along with the hay.

"Dear God," he cried, "however did I land in the gristmill!" But soon he fathomed where he was. Now he had to take pains not to land between two teeth and be crunched up, and thereafter he had to stay afloat, slithering along down into the stomach. "They forgot to put windows in this little room," he said. "No rays of sunlight shine in, nor did anyone fetch me a night-light." He found the lodgings altogether lacking, and worst of all, more and more hay kept coming through the door, and the space got ever tighter. Finally he cried out in terror as loud as he could, "Don't bring me any more feed, don't bring me any more feed!"

The maid was just milking the cow, and when she heard a voice without seeing anyone about, and fathomed that it was the same voice she had heard during the night, she took such fright she slipped off the milking stool and spilled the milk and ran as fast as she could to her master and cried, "For God's sake, reverend, sir, the cow just spoke."

"You've lost your mind," replied the pastor, but went to the cowshed to see for himself what's what.

But no sooner had he set foot inside than Tom Thumb cried out again, "Don't bring me any fresh feed, don't bring me any fresh feed."

Whereupon the pastor took fright, believing it to be an evil spirit that had entered the cow, and he decided to kill it. So the cow was slaughtered, but the stomach in which Tom Thumb lodged was tossed into the garbage heap. Tom Thumb had an awful time wriggling his way out, until he finally managed. But when he went to poke his head out, poor lad, he was engulfed by a new misfortune. A hungry wolf came running up and gobbled down the entire stomach in one gulp. But Tom Thumb never lost courage. Perhaps, he thought, I can bend the wolf's ear with my words, and he shouted out of the pit of the wolf's paunch, "Dear wolf, I know where you can find a tender tidbit."

"Where's that?" said the wolf.

"In a house on such and such a street, if you creep along the curb, you'll find cake, bacon, and sausage aplenty, as much as you can eat," and told him the way to his father's house. The wolf, not needing to be told twice, slunk along in the dark of night and ate his fill in the storeroom. Once he was full he wanted to slink off, but he had become so fat that he couldn't fit out the door again, which is just what Tom Thumb counted on. He promptly started making a prodigious racket in the wolf's gut, raging and roaring as loud as he could.

"Will you be quiet," said the wolf. "You'll wake everyone up."

"What's fair is fair," the little one replied. "You had your fill, now it's my turn to make merry," and he started screaming again at the top of his lungs.

The racket finally awakened his father and mother, who went running to the storeroom and peaked through a crack in the planks. As soon as they saw a wolf crouching within, they ran off. The man fetched an ax and the woman a scythe.

"Stand back," said the man as they entered the storeroom, "and once I heave to with a blow that stuns him, swing the scythe and cut him to pieces."

Then Tom Thumb heard his father's voice and cried, "Dear Father, I'm here, stuck in the body of the wolf."

Overjoyed, the father cried out, "Thank God, our beloved child is back," and had his wife stay the scythe so as not to harm Tom Thumb. But he heaved to again and struck the wolf with such a mighty blow to the head that it fell dead. Then the parents found a knife and shears, cut open the wolf's belly, and promptly pulled out their little son.

"Heaven help us," said the father, "we were worried to death about you!"

"Yes, Father, I did get around in the world. Thank God I can breathe fresh air again!"

"Whereabouts have you been?"

"Oh, Father, I've spent time in a mouse hole, in a cow's stomach, and in the wolf's gut. It's good to be home again."

"We wouldn't sell you again for all the riches in the world," said the parents, who kissed and cuddled their dear Tom Thumb. Then they gave him plenty to eat and drink, and made him a new suit of clothes, as his old duds were tattered from his travels.

FAITHFUL JOHANNES

. .
.

*O*nce upon a time there was an old king who fell ill and thought, The bed in which I lie will surely be my deathbed. So he said, "Tell Faithful Johannes to come to me." Faithful Johannes was his favorite servant, so called because he had faithfully served the king for his entire life. Once he stood before the bed, the king said to him, "Dear Faithful Johannes, I feel that my end is near, and my only worry is about my son – he is still so young he cannot always make decisions for himself, and if you do not promise me that you will counsel him in all he needs to know and be his foster father, I cannot die in peace."

To which Faithful Johannes replied, "I will not forsake him and will gladly serve him, even if it costs me my life."

Whereupon the old king said, "Then I can die in peace and confidence." And he added: "After my death, take him around the entire castle, to every chamber, hall, and vaulted passageway, and show him all the treasures it contains – but don't take him to the last chamber at the end of the long hallway in which the painting called *The Princess of the Golden Roof* lies hidden. If he lays eyes on that painting, he will be so smitten by her beauty that he will swoon and for her sake face great peril. You must safeguard him from that." And when Faithful Johannes once again shook hands on it, the king lay his head back on the pillow, was still, and died.

As they carried the old king out to be buried, Faithful Johannes told the young king what he had promised his father on his deathbed, and added: "On my honor I will keep my word, and be faithful to you as I was to him, even at the cost of my life."

Once the mourning period was over, Faithful Johannes said to him, "It is time for you to see your inheritance – I will show you around your father's castle." So he took him everywhere, up and down the keep, and showed him all of the magnificent chambers and the treasures they contained – all except for the room with the perilous painting. But the painting was positioned such that you saw it as soon as the door swung open, and it was so splendidly painted that the princess looked alive and kicking and there was nothing sweeter and lovelier to look upon in the whole wide world.

The young king noticed that Faithful Johannes always bypassed one doorway and said, "Why don't you unlock this one?"

"There is something terrible to look upon inside," he said.

But the young king replied, "I have seen the entire castle, so I want to know what's in there too." He lunged forward and wanted to force the door open.

But Faithful Johannes held him back and said, "I swore to your father on his deathbed that you would not set eyes on what's in there – it could bring you and me great misfortune."

"Stuff and nonsense," said the young king. "If I can't get in there it will be my undoing. Day and night I would not rest until I'd seen it with my own eyes. I will not move from this spot until you unlock that door."

Faithful Johannes fathomed that there was nothing to be done, and sighing with a heavy heart he searched for the right key on the big key chain. Once he had opened the door he entered first, intending to hide the painting so that the king would not see it, but it was no use. The king stood on tiptoes and spotted it over his shoulder. And no sooner did he catch a glimpse of the painting of the fair maiden glimmering with gold and precious stones than he fainted and fell to the ground. Faithful Johannes picked him up and carried him to his bed, fretting all the while. "Dear God, the thing is done, what misfortune will it bring us!"

Then he fortified the young king with a swallow of wine until he came to again. But the first words he said upon waking were: "Who, in heaven's name, is the girl in the painting?"

"She is the Princess of the Golden Roof," replied Faithful Johannes.

Then the king replied, "My love for her is so great, if all the leaves on the trees were tongues they could not express it. I will devote my life to finding her. You are my Faithful Johannes, you must stand by me."

Faithful Johannes pondered for a long while how to go about tackling this task, as it was hard enough just to stand there and peer at the princess's face. Finally he had an idea and said to the king, "Everything around her is made of gold – tables, chairs, bowls, goblets, pans, and all household utensils. There are four tons of gold in your treasure vault. Have one of the goldsmiths of your realm fashion it into all sorts of receptacles and devices, into birds, wild game, and wondrous golden creatures. That will please her, and we will carry it with us to her kingdom and try our luck."

The king had all the goldsmiths in his realm called to the palace and commanded them to work day and night until finally they had completed all the lovely things. Once everything was loaded onto a ship, Faithful Johannes dressed up as a merchant and bid the king do the same, so as to travel incognito. Then they shoved off across the sea and sailed a long way until they came to the city in which the Princess of the Golden Roof lived.

Faithful Johannes told the king to remain on the ship and wait for him. "Maybe," he said, "I'll bring the princess back with me. Make sure everything is in order, and have the gold receptacles brought up to the deck and decorate the entire ship." Thereupon he gathered all sorts of golden objects and stuffed them into the pockets of his smock, disembarked, and went straight to the royal palace. When he came to the palace courtyard, there before a well stood a beautiful girl with two golden buckets in hand with which she drew water. And when she turned around to carry off the sparkling water she saw the stranger and asked him who he was.

To which he replied, "I am a merchant," and he loosened the pockets of his smock and let her look in.

Whereupon she cried out, "Oh what lovely gold things!," put down the buckets, and examined them one by one. Then the girl said, "The princess must see this. She loves golden objects so much she will buy all of your wares." So she took him by the hand and led him up to see the princess, for the girl was her handmaiden. When the princess saw all the wares Faithful Johannes carried with him, she was delighted and said, "It is so finely fashioned that I will buy it all."

But Faithful Johannes replied, "I am only the servant of a wealthy merchant. What you see here is nothing compared to what my master has on his ship – the most artful and precious objects ever fashioned out of gold." She immediately wanted to have everything brought to her, but he said, "That would take many days, so great are they in number, and they would fill so many chambers that your castle would not suffice."

The princess's curiosity and yearning were stirred to such a degree that she finally said, "Take me to the ship. I will go myself to see your master's treasures."

So Faithful Johannes led her to the ship, overjoyed that his plan had worked,

and as soon as the king set eyes on her, he saw that her beauty in person surpassed that of her portrait and felt like his heart would burst in his breast. Then she boarded the ship, and the king led her into the hold. But Faithful Johannes stayed behind with the helmsman and bid him shove off. "Unfurl your sails that we may fly like a bird in the sky."

Meanwhile the king showed her all the golden pots, one by one; the bowls, goblets, and pans; the golden birds and wild game and all the wondrously fashioned golden animals. Examining it all took many hours, and in her joy she did not notice that the ship had set sail. After she had admired the last golden object, she thanked the merchant and wanted to go home, but when she got to the bow she saw that the ship was advancing full sail at high sea far from land.

"Heaven help me," she cried out in terror, "I've been deceived, kidnapped, and am at the mercy of a merchant. I would rather die!"

The king promptly grabbed her by the hand and said, "A merchant I am not but a king, no lesser by birth than you – yet if I resorted to a ruse to carry you off, my overwhelming love for you is to blame. The first time I saw your portrait I swooned with love." When the Princess of the Golden Roof heard this she felt comforted, and her heart went out to him, so that she gladly agreed to become his wife.

But it so happened while they were sailing the high seas that Faithful Johannes, who was seated at the fore playing music, spied three ravens flying overhead. So he stopped playing and listened to their conversation, for he understood their language.

The one cried out, "Hey, he's taking the Princess of the Golden Roof home."

"Right," replied the second, "but he hasn't got her yet."

To which the third countered, "Sure, he's got her, she's seated beside him on the ship."

Then the first started squawking again and cried, "A lot of good it'll do him!

As soon as they land, a reddish brown horse will come leaping toward him, and he will try to swing himself into the saddle and never see his ladylove again."

Said the second, "Is there no way to save him?"

"Oh, yes," said the first, "if another man mounts first, removes the musket from the halter, and with it shoots the horse dead, then the young king will be saved. But who knows that? And whoever knows it and says it, he will be turned to stone from his toes to his knees."

Then the second one said, "I know more. Even if the horse is slain the young king still won't keep his bride. Once they get to the castle they will find, lying in a bowl, an embroidered nuptial robe that looks as if it's woven out of silver and gold but is, in fact, made of brimstone and pitch, and whosoever puts it on will burn down to his marrow and bones."

Said the third, "Is there no rescue?"

"Oh, yes," replied the second, "if someone wearing gloves grabs the robe and flings it into the fire so that it burns, the king will be saved. But what's the use? Whoever knows it and tells it to him, he will have half his body, from the knees to the heart, turned to stone."

Then the third said, "I know even more. Even if the nuptial robe is burned, the young king still won't have his bride. After the wedding when the minstrels strike up the music and the young queen gets up to dance, she will suddenly turn pale and appear to drop dead, and if someone does not pick her up and immediately draw three drops of blood from her right breast and spit them out again, she will die. But if someone knows it and reveals what he knows, then he will turn to stone from his spine to his toes."

Once the ravens had finished their conversation they flew off, and Faithful Johannes understood every word, but from that moment on he was sad and still. If he kept all he'd heard from his master, the latter would come to a miserable end, but if he revealed it to him, he himself would forfeit his life.

Finally, after mulling it over, he said to himself, "I will save my master, even if it means my own undoing."

Once they reached land, things happened as the raven had predicted, and a splendid reddish-brown nag came leaping forward.

"Up an' at 'em," said the king, "he'll carry me back to my castle," and was about to mount, but Faithful Johannes beat him to it, swiftly swung himself into the saddle, pulled the musket out of the halter, and shot the nag dead.

Thereupon the king's other servants, who had it in for Johannes, cried out, "What a disgrace to kill the beautiful creature that was to carry the king back to his castle!"

But the king said, "Bite your tongues and let it be. He is my Faithful Johannes, who knows why he did it?"

Then they came to the castle, and there in the hall was a bowl with a nuptial robe lying in it that looked like it was made of silver and gold. The young king walked up and wanted to reach for it, but Faithful Johannes shoved him aside, grabbed it with gloves, swiftly brought it to the fireplace, and burned it.

The other servants once again started grumbling and said, "Will you get a load of that, now the guy even grabs and burns the king's nuptial robe!"

But the young king said, "Who knows why he did it? Let him be, he is my Faithful Johannes."

So the wedding was celebrated – the dance began, and the bride strode to the dance floor, but Faithful Johannes was ready and looked her in the eye. Suddenly she turned pale and collapsed as if she'd dropped dead. Whereupon he leapt forward, picked her up, and carried her to a bed chamber. There he lay her down, knelt before her, and sucked three drops of blood from her right breast and spit them out. Straightaway she breathed again and got better, but the young king looked on in stunned amazement and, not knowing why Faithful Johannes did what he had done, flew into a rage and cried, "Lock him up!"

The following morning Faithful Johannes was condemned to die and taken to the gallows, and when he stood there ready to meet his Maker, he said, "Every condemned man about to die may speak a final word. Might I too have that right?"

"Yes," said the king, "your request is granted."

Whereupon Faithful Johannes spoke up: "I have been falsely accused and always remained faithful to you," and he went on to tell how back at sea he had overheard the conversation of the ravens, and how, to save his master, he was obliged to do all that he had done.

Then the king said, "Oh, my Faithful Johannes. Reprieve! Reprieve! Take him down from there and set him free." But upon speaking his last words, Johannes fell dead, his body turned to stone.

The king and queen were deeply distraught, and the king said, "Oh how miserably have I rewarded such great faithfulness!" And he had the stone likeness lifted up and set beside his bed. Every time he saw it, he wept and said, "If only I could bring you back to life again, my Faithful Johannes." Time passed, and the queen gave birth to twins, two little sons, who grew up and were her pride and joy. Once, when the queen went to church and the two boys sat by their father and played, the king again peered in sadness at the stone likeness, sighed, and said, "Oh if only I could bring you back to life, my Faithful Johannes."

Whereupon the stone started speaking and said, "Yes, you can bring me back to life again, if you will sacrifice your nearest and dearest."

Then the king cried, "Everything I have in the world I would give for you."

Said the stone, "If with your own two hands you will hack off your children's heads and rub their blood on me, I will come back to life again."

The king took fright upon hearing that he was to kill his dearly beloved children with his own hands, but then he thought of the dead man's great fidelity and how Faithful Johannes had died for him. He pulled out his sword, and with his own hand hacked his children's heads off. And no sooner did he rub their blood on the stone than it came back to life, and Faithful Johannes stood there before him alive and well. He said to the king, "Your fidelity should not go unrewarded," and took the children's heads, set them back on their shoulders, rubbed them with their blood, whereupon they instantly leapt back to life, jumped around, and went on playing as though nothing had happened.

Now the king was overjoyed, and when he saw the queen coming he hid Faithful Johannes and the two children in a big cupboard. When she came in he said to her, "Did you pray in church?"

"Yes," she said, "but I couldn't stop thinking of Faithful Johannes, that we caused him such misery."

To which he replied, "Dear wife, we can bring him back to life again, but it will cost us our two little sons. We must sacrifice them."

The queen went pale and felt her heart break, but she said, "We owe him that, on account of his great fidelity."

Whereupon the king was well-pleased, for they were of one mind, and he went over and unlocked the cupboard, pulled out the children and Faithful Johannes, and said, "Praise God, he is saved, and we have our sons back," and he told her all that had happened. And they lived happily together until their dying day.

HANS MY HEDGEHOG

There once was a plowman who had money and land aplenty, but prosperous as he was, there was something missing in his life without which he could not be happy – he and his wife had no children. Oftentimes when he went to town with other farmers they kidded him and asked why he had no children. That made him angrier and angrier, and when he got home he would burst out: "I want to have a child, even if it's a hedgehog."

Then his wife gave birth to a child who was a hedgehog on the top and a boy on the bottom, and when she saw the child, she took fright and said, "You see, you brought a curse on us."

To which the man replied, "There's no use complaining. The boy must be baptized, but we'll never find a godfather."

Then the woman said, "What else can we name him but Hans My Hedgehog?"

Once the boy was baptized, the pastor said, "With his prickly quills, such a child can't sleep in a regular bed."

So they strew a tuft of straw behind the oven and placed Hans My Hedgehog on it. He could not suckle at his mother's breast, since he would have pricked her. So he lay there behind the oven for eight years, and his father grew tired of him and thought, If only he would die. But he did not die, he just kept lying there. Then it so happened that there was a market in town and the plowman wanted to go, so he asked his wife what he could bring her.

"A little meat and a couple of rolls for dinner," she said.

Then he asked the maid, who wanted a pair of slippers and a pair of embroidered stockings.

Finally he said to his son, "Hans My Hedgehog, what would you like?"

"Dearest Dad," the son replied, "bring me back a bagpipe."

And when the father returned from the market, he gave his wife the meat and rolls he'd bought for her, then he gave the maid the slippers and embroidered stockings, and finally he went behind the oven and gave Hans My Hedgehog his bagpipe. And when Hans My Hedgehog had the bagpipe in hand, he said, "Dearest Dad, go to the blacksmith and have him hammer horseshoes for the cock, then I'll ride away and never come back."

His father was glad to be rid of him, so he had the cock shod. When it was done, Hans My Hedgehog sat himself upon its back and rode off, also taking along some pigs and a donkey to watch over in the woods. And once they reached the woods, the cock with Hans My Hedgehog on its back fluttered up a tall tree, and there they sat for many years until the herd of pigs grew plentiful, and the father had no contact with his son. But when he sat perched in the tree, Hans my Hedgehog blew on his bagpipe and made music that was very beautiful to hear.

Once, a king who had lost his way came riding by and heard the music. Surprised by the sound of it, he sent a servant to have a look around and see where the music was coming from. The servant looked around, yet he saw nothing but a small creature perched up in a tree, which looked like a

weather-cock with a hedgehog seated on his back playing a bagpipe. Then the king told his servant to inquire why he sat there and if he could tell him the way back to his kingdom.

Whereupon Hans My Hedgehog climbed down from the tree and said he would show him the way if the king would grant him in writing the first thing he happened upon when he got home. The king thought, What's the difference? Hans My Hedgehog surely can't read, and I can write what I please. So the king took up a quill, dipped it in ink, and wrote something down, and once it was done Hans My Hedgehog showed him the way, and he got home safe and sound. But as soon as his daughter saw the king from afar, she was so overjoyed that she came running toward him and covered him in kisses. Then the king thought of Hans My Hedgehog and told her what had happened to him, and that he had pretended to promise in writing to give this curious creature whatever he first encountered when he got home, and the creature had been mounted on a cock, as though on a horse, and made beautiful music. But the king had written that he would not have it, convinced that in any case Hans My Hedgehog couldn't read it. The princess was well-pleased with this and said it was a good thing, since she had no intention of ever marrying a hedgehog.

But Hans My Hedgehog kept watching his donkey and his pigs, seated happily in the treetop, blowing on his bagpipe. It so happened that another king who had lost his way came riding by with his servants and footmen and didn't know how to get home again because the forest was so vast. He too heard the beautiful music from afar and said to one of his footmen to go have a look and find out where it came from. The footman went and stood under the tree and saw the weathercock with Hans My Hedgehog seated on its back. He asked him what he was up to.

"I'm guarding my donkey and pigs. But how can I help you?"

The footman said they had gotten lost and could not find their way back to their kingdom, and asked if he could show them the way. So Hans My Hedgehog climbed down with his cock and told the old king he would gladly show him the way if he would give him whatever he first encountered upon reaching his royal castle. The king agreed and put in writing that Hans My Hedgehog should have what he asked for. Once it was done, Hans rode ahead on his cock to show him the way, and the king was glad to get back home to his kingdom.

Now the king had an only daughter who was very beautiful and came running toward him, fell into his arms, and kissed him, overjoyed at her old father's safe return. And when she asked him where in the world he had been for so long, he told her how he had gotten lost and might never have made it home again, but while passing through a great forest he happened upon a curious individual, half hedgehog, half human, mounted on a cock and perched in a tall tree, playing beautiful music, who had helped show him the way home, in exchange for which, however, he had promised to give whatever in his kingdom he first encountered, and that, he was so very sorry to say, turned out to be his daughter. Whereupon she promised, for love of her old father, to go with the curious individual when he came acalling.

But Hans My Hedgehog kept tending his pigs, and the pigs spawned little piglets, and they became so plentiful that they filled the entire forest. Then Hans My Hedgehog didn't want to live in the forest any longer, and he sent word to his father that they should empty all the stalls in the village, for he would return with such a great herd that everyone who wanted a pig would have one to slaughter. His father was not pleased when he got wind of this, as he thought his son had long since died. But Hans My Hedgehog sat himself on the weathercock, drove the herd of pigs back to the village, and had them all slaughtered. Heavens, was there ever such hacking and butchering! You could hear the sound of it a full two-hours' ride away.

"Dearest Dad," Hans My Hedgehog said when it was all done, "have my weathercock shod again at the smithy, then I'll ride away and never return again." So the father had the cock shod again, happy to be rid of his strange son once and for all.

Hans My Hedgehog rode off to the first kingdom. There the king had ordered that if anyone came riding on a cock with a bagpipe in hand, he was to be shot, beaten, and stabbed, so that he never made it to the castle. When Hans My Hedgehog came riding up, guards with bayonets fell upon him, but he spurred on his cock, and it flew up over the gate and landed in front of the king's window, where he dismounted and cried out that the king should give him what he promised, or else he would kill the king and his daughter. Then the king convinced his daughter to go out to him to save their lives. So she dressed herself in white, and her father gave her a coach drawn by six strong horses, with lavishly attired livery, and loaded down with gold and precious goods. She mounted the carriage, and Hans My Hedgehog sat next to her, with his cock and his bagpipe on the seat beside him, bid farewell, and drove off, and the king thought he would never see his daughter again. But things didn't turn out as he thought they would, since no sooner had they driven a short distance out of town than Hans My Hedgehog pulled off her lovely clothes and poked her with his hedgehog quills until she was bloody all over, saying, "That's just repayment for you and your father's deception. Be off, I don't want you," and he chased her home, and she was scorned her livelong day.

But Hans My Hedgehog rode on his cock and with his bagpipe to the second kingdom to which he had shown the king the way home. The king had ordained that if someone meeting the description of Hans My Hedgehog presented himself, his guards should present arms, salute him, give him free entry to the city, and lead him to the royal palace. When the princess saw him she took fright on account of his odd appearance, but she thought to herself, No matter, I promised my father. So she welcomed Hans My Hedgehog, whereupon they were married, and he had to be seated at the king's table, with her by his side, and they ate and drank.

Come nightfall, when it was time to go to bed, she feared the prick of his quills, but he said she need not be afraid and that no harm would come to her. And he told the old king to call for four men to keep watch before their bedroom door. They were to light a big fire, and when he went into the bedroom and lay himself in bed, he would wriggle out of his hedgehog skin and lay it down before the bed – then the men were to nimbly leap forward, grab the skin, toss it in the fire, and stand by watching until it was completely consumed by the flames.

As soon as the church bell struck eleven he went into the bedroom, stripped off his hedgehog skin, and left it lying before the bed. Then the men came and snatched it up, and tossed it into the fire. Once the flames had disposed of it, he was released from the evil spell and lay there in bed, a human from head to toe, but he was black as coal, like he'd been burned. The king sent for his physician, who washed Hans My Hedgehog with salves and wiped him with balms, whereupon he was white and a fine young buck. When the princess saw that, she was pleased, and the next morning they awakened with joy, ate and drank, and the wedding was celebrated, and Hans My Hedgehog inherited the kingdom.

After some years had passed he rode with his wife to visit his father and said he was his son. His father said he had no son. He'd had one, but the boy was born with prickly quills like a hedgehog and had gone out into the world. Then the young man revealed his true identity, and his old father was pleased and went with him to his son's kingdom.

Now my fairy tale is done,
Go find yourself another one.

ALL-KIND-OF-HIDE

$\cdot \cdot \cdot$

There once was a king who had a wife with golden hair, and she was so lovely that the like of her could no longer be found on earth. It came to pass that she fell ill, and when she sensed that she would soon die she called the king to her bedside and said, "If after my death you wish to remarry, then take no woman who isn't as lovely as me, nor any who lacks the same golden hair. This you must promise me." After the king had promised to do as she wished, she closed her eyes and died.

For a long time the king was inconsolable and didn't think of taking another wife. But finally his court counselors spoke up: "There are no two ways about it, the king must marry again so that we have a queen."

So messengers were sent out far and wide to find a bride whose beauty was equal to that of the departed queen. But there was no woman to be found in the whole world, and even if they could have found one, there was none with the same golden hair. So the messengers returned without having accomplished their mission.

Now the king had a daughter who was just as lovely as her departed mother and had the same golden hair. When she grew up, one day the king looked at her and saw that she resembled in every way his departed wife, and suddenly he felt a powerful love for her. So he said to his court counselors, "I will marry my daughter, for she is the spitting image of my dead wife, and I can't find any other bride who is her equal."

When the counselors heard this they were appalled and said, "God forbade the father to marry his daughter. Nothing good can come of such a sin, and your kingdom will be dragged along into your ignominy."

His daughter was even more horrified when she heard of her father's resolve, but still hoped to dissuade him. "Before I can fulfill your wish, I must first have three dresses: one as golden as the sun, one as silvery as the moon, and one as sparkling as the stars. Furthermore, I demand a coat of a thousand kinds of fur and hides. Every creature in your realm must contribute a piece of its hide." She thought to herself, Such a wish is completely impossible to fulfill, and I will thereby dissuade my father from his evil intent.

But the king did not let up, and the handiest maidens in his realm were commanded to weave the three dresses: one as golden as the sun, one as silvery as the moon, and one as sparkling as the stars. And his hunters had to catch all the creatures in his realm and pull off a piece of its hide, out of which was made a coat of a thousand hides. At last when everything was done as he commanded, the king had them fetch the coat, and when it was spread out before him, he said, "The wedding will take place tomorrow."

When the princess saw that there was no more hope of bending her father's will, she decided to escape. That night, while the palace slept, she got up and took three things from her treasure chest: a golden ring, a golden spinning wheel, and a little golden reel. The three dresses as golden as the sun, as silvery as the moon, and as sparkling as the stars she stuffed into a nutshell, and she donned the coat of all kinds of hides and blackened her face and hands with soot. Then she commended herself to God's care, dashed out the door, and kept walking all night until she came to a great forest. And since she was tired, she crept inside a hollow tree trunk and fell asleep.

The sun rose, and she kept sleeping and went right on sleeping until broad daylight.

It so happened that another king to whom the forest belonged went hunting in it. When the dogs came to the tree, they sniffed about, ran around it, and barked. Whereupon the king said to his hunters, "Go have a look at what kind of game is hidden inside."

The hunters obeyed his command, and upon their return they reported: "In the hollow of the tree lies a wondrous creature the like of which we have never seen – its skin is covered with a thousand kinds of hide. It lies there fast asleep."

Said the king, "Go see if you can catch it alive, then bind it to your cart and bring it to me."

When the hunters touched the girl, she awakened riddled with fear and cried out to them, "I am a poor child forsaken by father and mother. Have pity on me and take me with you."

To which they replied, "All-Kind-of-Hide, we can use you in the kitchen. Just come with us and you can sweep the ashes." So they put her in the cart and drove her back to the king's castle. There they assigned her a little cubbyhole under the stairs where the sun never shone and said, "Little wild thing, you can sleep here." Then they sent her to work in the kitchen, to carry wood and water, stoke the fire, pluck poultry feathers, tend to the vegetables, sweep the ashes, and to do all the lowliest tasks.

All-Kind-of-Hide lived quite miserably in this way for a long time. Oh, you lovely princess, what, pray tell, will become of you! But one day it so happened that they threw a party in the castle, so she said to the cook, "May I go up for a little while to watch? I'll stay outside and just peek in through the open door."

Said the cook, "Sure, go ahead, but in half an hour you must be back to gather up the ashes."

Whereupon she took her little oil lamp, went to her little cubbyhole, took off the coat of many hides, and washed the soot off her face and hands, and there she stood again in all her loveliness. Then she opened her nutshell and pulled out her gown, the one that shone as golden as the sun. Once dressed, she went up to the party, and everyone made way for her, as no one recognized her, and they all thought she must surely be a princess. But the king came toward her, reached out his hand to dance with her, and thought to himself, Never have my eyes seen a creature so lovely. When the dance was done, she bowed, and no sooner did the king turn to look than she was gone, and no one knew where. The guards posted outside the castle gates were summoned and interrogated, but not a one had seen her.

She had rushed back to her little cubbyhole, swiftly slipped out of her dress, blackened her face and hands, donned the rough coat, and was again All-Kind-of-Hide. When she returned to the kitchen to resume her work, intending to sweep up the ashes, the cook said, "That can wait until tomorrow. Boil me up the king's soup – I too would like to take a peek at the festivities – but don't let a hair fall in, or else you'll get nothing more to eat."

So the cook headed to the party, and All-Kind-of-Hide boiled up the king's soup, a bread soup, as tasty as can be, and when it was done she went to her little cubbyhole to fetch the golden ring and dropped it in the king's soup bowl. When the ball was over the king called for his soup and ate it, and it tasted so good he thought he had never tasted a soup quite so delicious. But when he got to the bottom of the bowl he saw a golden ring and couldn't fathom how it got there. So he commanded the cook to appear before him. The cook took fright and said to All-Kind-of-Hide, "I bet you let a hair drop in the soup. If you did I'll skin your hide."

When the cook appeared before the king, His Majesty asked who boiled up the soup.

Said the cook, "I did."

But the king said, "It cannot be, for it's not the soup I'm accustomed to. It's boiled up much better than usual."

Whereto the cook replied, "I must confess, it was not I who boiled it up but the wild child."

Said the king, "Go and bid her appear before me."

When All-Kind-of-Hide came up, the king asked, "Who are you?"

"I am a poor child forsaken by father and mother."

"What are you doing in my castle?" he asked.

"I'm good for nothing but to have boots hurled at my head."

"Where did you get the ring I found in my soup?" he sounded her out.

Whereto she replied, "I know nothing of the ring."

Frustrated, the king sent her away.

Time passed and the king once again threw a party. As before, All-Kind-of-Hide asked the cook's permission to take a peek.

"Yes," said the cook, "but be back in half an hour to boil up the bread soup that the king likes so much."

So she ran to her little cubbyhole, washed herself up lickety-split, and took from the nutshell and donned the dress as silvery as the moon. Then she went up, resplendent as a princess, and the king came toward her, glad to see her again, and as the ball was just starting they danced together. But when the dance was done she disappeared so fast the king had no idea where she went. She scampered back to her little cubbyhole, made herself back up as the wild child, and went to the kitchen to boil up the bread soup. Once the cook was out of sight, she fetched the golden spinning wheel, dropped it in the bowl, and poured the soup all over it. Whereupon the soup was served to the king, who ate it, and he liked it as much as he had the last time. So he once again called for the cook, who once again had to confess that it was All-Kind-of-Hide who had boiled it up. And again she appeared before the king, but she replied that she was good for nothing but to have boots hurled at her head, and that she knew nothing of the golden spinning wheel.

When the king threw a third party, things went pretty much the same as they had before. Though this time the cook said, "You must be a witch, wild child, always adding something to the soup that makes it taste better to the king than what I cook him." But because she pleaded with him, he finally let her go up for a short time to take a peek at the party. This time she put on her dress that was as sparkling as the stars and, so attired, strode into the ballroom. Again the king danced with the lovely maiden and thought that she looked lovelier than ever. And mid-dance, without her noticing it, he slipped a golden ring onto her finger, and he ordered that the dance last a long while. Once the dance was done, he wanted to hold her fast in his hands, but she tore herself free of his grip and leapt so quickly among the other guests that she disappeared before his very eyes. She ran as fast as she could to her little cubbyhole beneath the stairs, but because she'd stayed away so long, more than the half-hour leave the cook had allowed her, she had no time to take off the lovely gown but just drew her coat of many hides over it, and in her haste she failed to apply enough soot, leaving one finger white. In this state All-Kind-of-Hide ran to the kitchen, cooked the king his bread soup, and once the cook was gone, dropped the little golden reel in the soup. When the king found it at the bottom of his bowl he called for All-Kind-of-Hide – whereupon he spotted the white finger and the gold ring he'd slipped on it during the dance. So he grabbed hold of her hand and held it tight, and when she struggled to break free, the coat of many hides split open and the dress that was as sparkling as the stars shimmered forth. The king grabbed hold of the coat and tore it off.

Whereupon her golden hair spilled out, and she stood there in all her beauty and could no longer disguise herself. And once she had wiped all the soot and ash from her face, she was lovelier than ever there was a woman on earth.

Then the king said, "You are my beloved bride, and we will never again part." Then the wedding was celebrated, and they lived happily together until their dying day.

THE SEVEN RAVENS

A man had *seven sons* and still not a single little daughter, as much as he hoped for one. At last his wife announced that she was once again expecting, and when the child was born, it was indeed a girl. The father's joy was great, but the child was frail and small, and on account of her frailty was to be baptized posthaste lest she die. The father bid one of his sons rush to the well to fetch water for the baptism The other six ran after him, and because each of them wanted to be the first to draw the water, they dropped the jug into the well. Whereupon they stood around, not knowing what to do, and not a one dared go home. When they didn't show up, the father grew impatient and said, "I'll bet they got caught up in a game and forgot, the godless lads." He was afraid the girl would die before being baptized, and in his anger he cried out, "I wish those no-good boys would all turn into ravens!" No sooner were the words spoken than he heard a crowing in the sky overhead, looked up, and saw seven coal-black ravens fly away.

The parents could no longer take back the malediction, and as sad as they were about the loss of their seven sons, they found some solace in their dear daughter, who soon rallied and grew more beautiful every day. For a long time the girl did not even know that she had any siblings, as the parents took pains not to mention them, until one day she overheard people speaking about her. The girl was lovely to look at, they said, but she was, after all, the cause of her seven brothers' misfortune. Greatly saddened, she went to her father and mother and asked them if she did indeed have brothers, and what had become of them. Now the parents could no longer keep the secret, but told her that fate had wanted it to be so, and that her birth was just a catalyst, not the cause. Nevertheless, every day the girl blamed herself and believed that it was up to her to free them from the spell. She could not rest easy, so one day she opened the door and went out into the world to track down her brothers and free them, whatever it might take. She took nothing with her but a little ring her parents had given her as a keepsake, a loaf of bread to still her hunger, a jug of water to slake her thirst, and a little stool for when she got tired.

She kept on walking, farther and farther, all the way to the end of the world. She came to the sun, but the sun was too hot and terrible and consumed little children for lunch. So the girl ran away as fast as she could and ran to the moon, but the moon was too cold and just as gruesome and evil, and no sooner did it notice the presence of the child than it said, "I smell human flesh."

So the girl made tracks and came to the stars. They were friendly and good and each one sat on his own little stool. But the morning star stood up, gave her a little chicken bone, and said, "If you don't have this little chicken bone you can't unlock the Glass Mountain, and that's where your brothers are."

The girl took the little bone, wrapped it in a little cloth, and kept on walking until she came to the Glass Mountain. The gate was locked and she wanted to take out the bone, but when she unfolded the cloth there was nothing in it. She had lost the gift of the good stars. So what was she to do now? She wanted to save her brothers and had no key to unlock the Glass Mountain. The good little sister took a knife, cut off her little finger, stuck it in the hole, and the lock clicked open. As soon as she went in a dwarf approached her and said, "My child, what are you searching for?"

"I'm searching for my brothers, the seven ravens," she replied.

The dwarf said, "Messrs. Ravens aren't home, but if you'd like to wait for them to return, you're welcome to come in." Thereupon the dwarf brought in the ravens' food on seven little plates, and their water in seven little cups, and the little sister ate a crumb from each little plate and took a swallow from each little cup. But in the last little cup she dropped the little ring she'd brought along.

Then all of a sudden she heard a whirring and whizzing, whereupon the dwarf said, "Messrs. Ravens are flying home."

So they came swooping in, wanted to eat and drink, and searched for their little plates and little cups. One after another they said, "Who has eaten from my little plate? Who has drunk from my little cup? It must have been a human mouth."

And when the seventh raven got to the bottom of his cup a little ring rolled out. He looked it over and recognized that it was a ring that belonged to their father and mother, and said, "God willing, if only our little sister were here, then we'd be saved."

When the girl, who was hiding behind the door, listening, heard that wish spoken, she stepped out from behind the door, and the ravens all got their human form back. And they hugged and kissed each other and happily hurried home.

THE LEAPING, PEEPING LITTLE LION'S LARK

There once was a man about to set out on a long journey, and upon taking leave he asked his three daughters what they would like him to bring back as a gift. The eldest wanted pearls, the middle daughter wanted diamonds, the youngest said, "Dear Father, I would like a leaping, peeping little lion's lark."

The father said, "If I can find it, it's yours," then kissed all three goodbye and started on his way. When the time came for him to return home, he had bought the pearls and the diamonds for the two elder sisters, but he had sought in vain for the leaping, peeping little lion's lark for the youngest, and he felt bad about it because he loved her the most of all. The way home led through a forest, and in the midst of the forest stood a splendid castle, and beside the castle stood a tree, and at the top of the tree, he spotted a leaping, peeping little lion's lark. "You're just what the doctor ordered," he said, overjoyed, and ordered his servant to climb up and catch the little creature.

But as the servant approached the tree, a lion leapt out from behind the trunk, reeled with anger, and roared so loud the leaves trembled on the branches. "He who tries to steal my leaping, peeping little lion's lark," he roared, "I'll have for lunch!"

Then the father said, "I didn't know the bird belonged to you. I'll make it up to you with silver and gold, if only you spare my life."

The lion said, "Nothing can save you, unless you promise to let me have who- or whatever first you meet when you get home. If you agree, I'll spare your life and let you have the bird for your daughter to boot."

The man hesitated and said, "It could be my youngest daughter, since she loves me the most and always comes running when I get home."

But the servant was frightened and said, "Who says it has to be your daughter you meet first? It could just as well be a cat or a dog."

So the father let himself be persuaded, took the leaping, peeping little lion's lark with him, and promised to let the lion have what first he met when he got home.

As soon as he got home and stepped into his house, who should come running but his youngest, dearest daughter. She kissed and cuddled him, and when she saw that he had brought her a leaping, peeping little lion's lark she was beside herself with joy. But the father, feeling no joy, burst out in tears and said, "My most beloved child, the little bird cost me dearly. I had to promise you in exchange to a wild lion, and when he has you he will tear you to shreds and devour you." And he told her everything that had happened and begged her not to go to the lion, come what may.

But she comforted him with these words: "Dear Father, the promise you made must be kept. I will go there, and don't worry, somehow I'll manage to pacify the lion, and I'll return hail and healthy back to you."

The next morning she had him show her the way, bid farewell, and went with good cheer into the forest. The lion, as it turned out, was a bedeviled

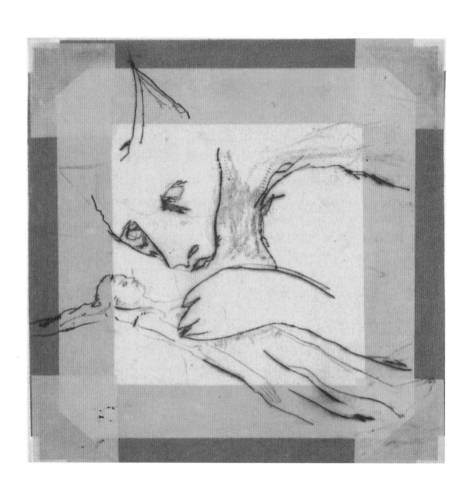

prince, a lion by day, and all his retinue had been turned into lions, but at night they resumed their human shape. Upon her arrival she was warmly received and shown into the castle. When night fell he was a handsome man, and the wedding was celebrated with great pomp. They lived happily together, awake at night, and asleep by day.

One day he came to her and said, "Tomorrow there will be a big celebration in your father's house. Your eldest sister's getting married, and if you wish to attend, my lions will take you there."

Yes, she said, she would very much like to see her father again, and rode there with a retinue of lions. Everyone was overjoyed to see her, since they thought she had been torn to shreds by lions long ago. But she told them what a handsome husband she had and how happy she was and stayed until the end of the wedding festivities, whereupon she returned to the forest.

When her second sister was to be married and she was once again invited to the wedding, she said to the lion, "This time I don't want to go alone. You must come with me."

But the lion said it would be too risky for him, for were he to be struck by a beam of burning light he would be transformed into a dove and would have to spend seven years flying with the doves.

"Oh," she said, "just come along. I'll watch over you and guard you from the glimmer of any light."

So they set out together and took along the little child who had been born to them.

She had a hall built with walls so strong and thick that not a ray of light could burst in. But the door was made of freshly hewn wood, and it sprung a tiny fissure no eye could see.

Now the marriage was celebrated with great pomp, but on the wedding party's way back from the church, all lit up with torches and lanterns, as they passed the hall a hair's breadth flicker of light fell on the prince, and as soon as it grazed him, at that very moment he was transformed. When she came in looking for him, he was nowhere in sight, but in his place she found a snow-white dove.

The dove spoke to her: "For seven years must I fly around the world, but every seven flaps I will let a red drop of blood and a white feather fall. They will show you the way, and if you follow my path you can break the spell."

Whereupon the dove flew out the door and she followed, and every seven flaps a drop of red blood and a snow-white feather fell and showed her the way. So she went out into the big wide world, never looking about, never resting, until almost seven years had elapsed. She rejoiced, thinking his redemption was so close, and yet it was still so far.

Once, as she went walking, no feather fell and no drop of red blood, and when she looked about she saw that the dove had disappeared. And as she thought, Humans cannot help me here, she climbed up to the sun and said to it, "You shine through every rift and over every spire. Did you not see a white dove flying by?"

"No," said the sun, "no white dove did I see, but here's a little chest. Open it when you're in great need."

She thanked the sun and she kept walking until evening when the moon appeared. Then she asked the moon, "You shine the whole night long, and over all the fields and forests of the world. Did you not see a white dove flying by?"

"No," said the moon, "no white dove did I see, but here's an egg. Break it when you're in great need."

She thanked the moon and kept on walking until the Night Wind came blowing by, and she said, "You blow over all the trees and under every leaf. Did you not see a white dove flying by?"

"No," said the Night Wind, "no white dove did I see, but I will ask the three other winds, perhaps they saw it."

The East Wind and the West Wind blew by, but they hadn't seen it. But the South Wind said, "Yes, I did see the white dove. It flew to the Red Sea, and there it turned into a lion again, since the seven years were up, and the lion is doing battle with a dragon, which is an enchanted princess."

Then the Night Wind spoke to her: "I'll give you a word of advice. Go to the Red Sea. On the right bank you'll find stalks of cane growing. Count them and cut off the eleventh stalk, and with it strike the dragon, then the lion can subdue it, and both will get their human bodies back. After that look around, and you'll find the griffin who sits on the Red Sea. Swing yourself with your beloved on his back, and he will fly you both home. Here, take this walnut, and when you're midway across the water, let if fall, and a great big walnut tree will rise out of the deep, on which the griffin will rest, for if he could not rest he would not be strong enough to carry you across and if you forget to drop the nut he'll shake you off into the Red Sea."

She walked on and found everything just as the Night Wind said she would. She counted the stalks of cane growing by the sea and cut the eleventh stalk off, and with it struck the dragon, and the lion subdued it. At that very instant the two regained their human forms. But as soon as the princess who had previously been a dragon was freed from her spell, she took the young man in her arms, climbed onto the griffin, and flew off with him. Now the poor girl who had traveled far and wide was abandoned again and she sat down and wept. But finally she pulled herself together and said, "I will walk as far as the wind blows and as long as I can still hear the rooster crow until I find him."

And she walked away, and kept walking a long, long way, until at last she came to the castle where the two of them, the dragon princess and her lion king, lived. She heard that there would soon be a festivity at which the two were to be wed. Whereupon she said, "God will still help me," and took out the little chest that the sun had given her, and in it there was a dress as radiant as the sun itself.

So she took it out and put it on and went into the castle, and everyone, including the bride, was struck by her appearance. The bride took such a fancy to it that she thought it would make a wonderful wedding gown, and asked if it might not be for sale.

"Not for gold or goods," the girl replied, "but for flesh and blood."

The bride asked her what she meant by that.

The girl said, "Let me spend a night in the chamber where the bridegroom sleeps."

The bride was reluctant at first, but she so badly wanted the dress that she finally gave in, under the condition that the valet give the prince a sleeping potion.

When night fell and the prince already lay asleep, the girl was led into the chamber. She sat on the edge of the bed and said, "I followed you for seven long years, went to the sun, the moon, and the four winds to ask after you, and I helped you subdue the dragon. Pray tell me, my prince, how then can you forget me?"

But the prince slept so soundly that it only seemed to him as if what he heard were the wind wafting outside in the evergreens. At daybreak she was led out of the chamber and had to hand over her golden dress. Fathoming that it was all for naught, she was sad, went outside, sat on a lawn, and wept. But as she sat there she remembered that she still had the egg the moon had given her. She cracked it open and out came a golden clucking hen with twelve little golden chicks that ran around and peeped and crept back under their mother's wings, and there was no lovelier sight in this world. Then she stood up and drove them along the lawn until the bride looked out her window and was so taken by the little golden chicks that she came running out and asked if they might not be for sale.

"Not for gold and goods, but for flesh and blood. Let me spend another night in the bedchamber of the sleeping prince."

The bride agreed, intending to trick her as she had the previous night. But when the prince went to bed he asked his valet what all the muttering and murmuring was about last night. The valet told him everything, that he had been told to slip him a sleeping potion because a poor girl spent the night in secret in his chamber, and tonight he was told to do the same.

The prince said, "Pour the potion out beside my bed."

That night the girl was let in again, and as soon as she started to tell how badly things had gone for her, he immediately recognized the voice of his beloved wife, leapt up, and cried, "Only now am I truly released from the spell. It was like in a dream, for the strange princess held me in her thrall and made me forget all about you, but God delivered me from my delusion in the nick of time." Together they snuck out of the castle in the dark of night, for they feared the princess's father, an evil sorcerer, and sat themselves on the griffin, who carried them across the Red Sea. And when they reached the middle of the sea, she let a walnut fall. And instantly a tall walnut tree grew out of the water, on which the griffin rested and then flew them home, where they found their child, who had since grown big and beautiful, and from then on they lived happily together until their dying day.

THE GIRL WITH NO HANDS

A miller fell little by little into poverty and soon had nothing left but his mill and the big apple tree that stood behind it. One day he went walking in the forest to gather wood, and an old man he had never seen before approached him and said, "Why break your back cutting wood? I can make you rich, if only you promise to give me what's standing behind the mill." What else could it be than the apple tree? the miller thought, so he said yes and signed it over to the stranger. Whereupon the latter cackled and said, "In three years' time I'll be back to pick up what's mine," and walked away.

When the miller got home, his wife came running to him and said, "Tell me, husband, where does all our wondrous wealth come from? All of a sudden our trunks and cabinets are full to bursting. Nobody brought it in, and I have no idea where it came from."

To which he replied, "It comes from the stranger I met in the forest who promised me great wealth in exchange for which I signed over possession to what's standing behind the mill – the big apple tree is small recompense for such a windfall."

"Oh, husband," replied his horrified wife, "that was the Devil – he didn't mean the apple tree but our daughter, who happened to be standing behind the mill sweeping up the yard."

The miller's daughter was a beautiful and God-fearing girl, who whiled away the three years in piety and without sin. When the time was up and the day came on which the Evil One wanted to fetch her, she washed herself clean from head to toe and drew a circle around herself with chalk. The Devil came acalling early, but he could not draw near her. In a fury he said to the miller, "Take all the water away from her so she can't wash herself anymore, or else I can't make her mine."

The miller was terrified and did what he was told. The next morning the Devil returned, but the girl had cried on her hands, washing them clean with her tears. Again he could not draw near. In a rage he said to the miller, "Hack off her hands, or else I can't make her mine."

Appalled, the miller replied, "How can I hack off my own child's hands!"

But the Evil One threatened him in a menacing voice: "If you don't do it, you're done for, and I will come and fetch you myself."

Terror-struck, the father promised to obey. Then he went to his daughter and said, "My child, if I don't hack off your hands the Devil will take me away, and in a fit of fear I promised I would. Help me in my need and forgive me for what I must do to you."

To which she replied, "Dear Father, do with me what you will, I'm your child." Whereupon she stretched both her hands before her and let them be hacked off. Now the Devil came a third time, but she had wept so long and so much on her stumps that they were washed clean. So he had to relent and lost all claim to her.

The miller said to her, "You have brought me such great gain. I will care for you and keep you in the lap of luxury your whole life."

But she replied, "I can't stay here. I have to go away – kindhearted people will surely give me what I need."

Whereupon after having the stumps of her mutilated arms tied to her back, she set out at dawn and walked the whole day until nightfall. She found herself at the edge of a royal garden and saw in the moonlight that the trees were ripe with luscious fruit, but she could not enter, as the garden was ringed by a moat. And because she had walked the whole day without a bite to eat and hunger gnawed at her gut, she thought to herself, If only I could get into the garden to eat of the fruit, or else I will surely die. So she knelt down, called out, and prayed to God the Father. All at once an angel appeared and built a sluice in the moat so that the water drained off, the bed went dry, and she could walk across. Then she entered the garden and the angel went with her. She saw a fruit tree full with luscious-looking pears, but they all belonged to the king. She stepped forward and bit into one, only one, straight off the tree to still her hunger. The gardener was watching, but because the angel stood by her, he was afraid, and thinking the girl must be a ghost, he kept still and dared not address her. Once she'd eaten the pear and her hunger was stilled, she went and hid behind a bush.

The following morning, the king to whom the garden belonged came to count the pears and noticed that one was missing. He asked the gardener what had become of it, since he could not see it lying under the tree. The gardener replied, "Last night, sire, a ghost with no hands bit one straight off the tree."

The king said, "How did the ghost get across the moat? And where did he go after eating the pear?"

The gardener replied, "Someone in a snow-white gown came down from the sky and built a sluice to drain off the water so that the ghost could walk across. And since it must have been an angel, I took fright and didn't dare object. As soon as the ghost ate the pear he went away again."

To which the king replied, "If what you say is true, I'll stand guard with you tonight."

When darkness fell, the king came into the garden and brought a priest along to speak to the ghost. The three of them sat under the tree and waited. At midnight the girl crept out from behind the bush, approached the tree, and gnawed off another pear with her teeth. The angel in white was standing beside her.

Now the priest stepped forward and said, "Are you God-sent or of this world? Are you ghost or mortal?"

To which she replied, "I am no ghost, but a poor lost soul, forsaken by all but the Lord."

The king said, "If you are forsaken by all, I will not forsake you." He took her along with him into his castle, and because she was so pretty and pious, he loved her with all his heart, had silver hands fashioned for her, and took her as his wife.

A year passed and the king had affairs to attend to far afield. So he left the young queen in the care of his mother and said, "When she is ready to bear me a child, take good care of her and make quick to send me a dispatch."

It came to pass that she gave birth to a beautiful boy. Whereupon the king's old mother made haste to send him the glad tidings. But along the way the messenger rested beside a stream, and because he was so tired, he promptly fell asleep.

Now the Devil, who had long born a grudge against the pious queen, appeared and exchanged the letter for another that said that the queen had given birth to a changeling. No sooner did the king read the letter than he was horrified and fell into a deep depression, but he wrote back that the queen should be well cared for until his return. The messenger returned with the letter, rested at the same spot along the way, where he once again fell asleep.

Whereupon the Devil dropped by again, took the letter from the messenger's pouch, and replaced it with another that said the queen and the child should be killed. Upon reading it, the old mother was stunned and could not believe her eyes. She wrote back to the king again, but each time the Devil switched letters – and in the last one it said that the queen's eyes and tongue were to be cut out and kept as proof of her execution.

Horrified at the thought of shedding such innocent blood, the old mother had a doe hunted down that night and cut out her tongue and eyes to keep for the king. Then she said to the young queen, "I cannot have you killed, as the king commands, but you can't stay here any longer. Go with your child out into the world and never return." She bound the child onto his mother's back and the poor woman went away weeping. She came to a big, wild woods. There she knelt down and prayed to God, and the Lord's angel appeared and led her to a little house on which hung a little sign with the words: "All are free to enter." Out the door came a snow-white maiden who said, "Welcome, Your Highness," and led her in. She unbound the boy from off the poor woman's back and put him to her breast, so that he might drink, and lay him in a soft white bed.

Whereupon the woman said to the maiden, "How do you know that I am a queen?"

To which the maiden replied, "I am an angel sent by God to care for you and your child."

And the woman remained seven years in the little house, where she was cared for and fed, and because of her piety, by the mercy of God her hacked-off hands grew back.

The king finally returned to his castle, and his first wish was to see the queen and the child. Then his old mother started crying and said, "You evil man, did you not write, commanding me to take two innocent lives?" And she showed him the two letters the Evil One had falsified, and continued: "I did as you ordered," and showed him as proof the tongue and eyes.

Then the king cried such bitter tears over his poor wife and little son that his old mother took mercy on him and said, "It's all right, she still lives! I had a doe slaughtered in her place and kept the tongue and eyes, but I bound the child on your wife's back and sent them out into the world, and made her promise never to come back, on account of your wrath."

To which the king replied, "I will search far and wide, and not eat or drink until I find my beloved wife and little son, if they have not already died of hunger."

Whereupon the king set out, and for seven long years he searched for her in vain on every cliff and in every cave, and thought for sure she must have perished. He did not eat or drink during that whole time, but God looked after him. Finally he came to a big, wild wood in which he found a little house with a little sign that said: "All are free to enter."

Then the maiden in white emerged, took him by the hand, led him in, and said, "Welcome, Your Majesty!" And she asked him where he came from.

"I have wandered a full seven years in search of my wife and child, but I cannot find them."

The angel bid him eat and drink, but he declined and only wished to rest for a while. Then he lay down to sleep and she covered his face with a cloth.

Then the angel went into the room where sat the queen and her son, whom she called Son of Misery. And the angel said to her, "Go out with your child – your husband has come."

Then the woman went to where he lay, and the cloth fell from his face. And she said to the boy, "Son of Misery, pick up the cloth from the floor and put it back over your father's face."

The child picked it up and put it back over the king's face.

The king heard all this in his half slumber and gladly let the cloth fall again.

Then the little boy grew impatient and said, "Dear Mother, how can I cover my father's face when I have no father in this world? I learned to pray 'Our Father who art in heaven,' and you told me my father was in heaven, and he was God Himself – so how am I to recognize this wild-eyed man?"

As soon as the king heard these words, he sat up and asked who the woman was.

"I am your wife," she said, "and that is your boy, Son of Misery."

Then he saw her flesh-and-blood hands and said, "My wife has silver hands."

And she replied, "God in His mercy let me grow back the real ones."

And the angel went into the room next door and fetched the silver hands and showed them to him.

Then the king knew for sure that it was his beloved wife and his dear child, and overjoyed, he kissed them and said, "A heavy stone has fallen from my heart."

Then the angel of God fed them again, and they went back home to the king's old mother. And there was great joy in the kingdom, and the king and queen celebrated a second wedding, and they lived together in happiness to a ripe old age.

RUMPELSTILZCHEN

O*nce upon a time* there was a poor miller who had a lovely daughter. Now it came to pass that he happened to speak to the king, and to give himself airs, he said, "I have a daughter who can spin straw into gold."

The king said to the miller, "That's an art that strikes my fancy. If your daughter is indeed as skillful as you say, bring her to my castle, and I'll put her to the test." When the girl was brought to him he led her to a room filled to the rafters with straw, gave her a spinning wheel and a reel, and said, "Now get to work, and if by morning you haven't spun this straw into gold, you will die." Whereupon he shut her in and left her alone.

So the poor miller's daughter sat there and did not for the life of her know what to do. She had no idea how to spin straw into gold, and she was soon in such a tizzy that she started to cry. Then all at once the door flew open and in stepped a little man who said, "Good evening, Miss Miller, why are you crying your eyes out?"

"Oh," replied the girl, "I'm supposed to spin straw into gold and have no idea how to do it."

Said the little man, "What will you give me if I do it for you?"

"I'll give you my necklace," said the girl.

The little man took her necklace, sat himself before the wheel, and lickety-split, in no time at all, the spool was full. Then he inserted more straw, and lickety-split, in no time at all the second one was full too – and so it went until morning, when all the straw was spun and all the spools were full of gold. At daybreak the king came by, stunned and delighted at the sight of all that gold. But his heart was greedy for more. He had the miller's daughter brought to a bigger room full of straw, and ordered her, if she valued her life, to spin it all into gold. The girl was so distraught that she started crying again, and once again the door flew open, and the little man appeared and said, "What will you give me if I spin the straw into gold?"

"I'll give you the ring from my finger," she replied.

So the little man took the ring, and once again started spinning the wheel, and by morning had spun all the straw into gold.

The king was overjoyed at the sight of it but hadn't yet had his fill, so he had the miller's daughter brought to a still-larger room filled with straw. "This night," said he, "you must spin it all – if you succeed I will take you as my wife." Even if she's only a miller's daughter, he thought to himself, I won't find a richer wife in the whole wide world.

When the girl sat there alone, the little man came to her a third time and said, "What will you give me if yet again I spin all this straw into gold?"

"I have nothing left to give you," said the girl.

"Then promise me once you're queen to give me your first child."

Who knows how all this will end, thought the miller's daughter, but with no other way out, she promised him what he asked, and in exchange the little man once again spun the straw into gold. When the king came the next morning and found all that he had asked for, he took her as his bride, and the lovely miller's daughter became his queen.

A year later she bore a beautiful child and never gave a thought to the little man, when, all at once, he strode into the room and said, "Now give me what you promised."

Now the queen took fright and offered the little man all the riches in the realm, if he would only leave her child. But the beastly little man said, "Not on your life! A living thing is dearer to me than all the treasures in the world." Then the queen started weeping and wailing so hard that the little man took pity on her. "I'll give you three days' time," he said, "and if by then you manage to find out my name, you can keep your child."

All night long the queen racked her brain over all the names she had ever heard, and she sent a messenger throughout the land to inquire far and wide after other names. When the little man came the next day, she began with Kasper, Melchior, Balthazar, and rattled off all the names she knew, one after the other, but each time the little man said, "Guess again."

The next day she sent her messenger to ask around what people were called in the neighboring lands, and when the little man appeared, she recited the oddest and strangest names: "Might you perchance be called Sparerib or Muttonchop or Lambshanks?"

But to each the little man responded, "Guess again."

On the third day the messenger returned and said, "No new names have I found, but at the edge of a forest at the foot of a high mountain in the middle of nowhere I spotted a little house, and in front of the house a fire burned, and by the fire leapt a paltry little man, skipping around on one foot and croaking:

'Today I bake, tomorrow I sup,
The next day I fetch the queen's young pup;
Never ever will she dream,

That Rumpelstilzchen is my name.'"

You can well imagine how overjoyed the queen was to hear that name, and when, a short while later, the little man returned and asked, "So, Your Majesty, what's my name?," she first asked, "Is it Kunz?"

"No."

"Is it Heinz?"

"No."

"Might your name perchance be Rumpelstilzchen?"

"Who the devil told you? Who the devil told you?" shrieked the little man, and in a furious fit stamped the ground so hard with his right foot that he got stuck up to the waist, whereupon, enraged, he took his left foot in both his hands and tore himself in two.

had the girl found her hiding place than the godless gang got home. They had dragged along another girl, were dead drunk, and kept on screaming and yammering. They gave her wine to drink, three glasses full – a glass of white, a glass of red, and a glass of yellow wine – which made her heart burst. They tore off her fine clothes, lay her on a table, chopped her lovely body into bits, and sprinkled it with salt. The poor bride hidden behind the barrel quaked and trembled with terror, for she saw what fate the robbers had in store for her. One of them noticed a golden ring on the little finger of the murdered girl, and since he could not slip it off, he took a cleaver and hacked the finger off, but the force of the blow made the severed finger bounce in the air and bound over the barrel, landing smack-dab in the bride's lap. The thief took a lantern and searched for it, but he couldn't find it. Whereupon another one said, "Have you looked behind the great big barrel?"

But the old woman called out, "Come and eat, and leave the looking for tomorrow – the finger won't run away."

"The old woman's right," the robbers replied, then left off their search and sat down to eat. The old woman dripped a sleeping potion into their wine, so that they soon lay down on the cellar floor and fell asleep. When the bride heard the sound of their snoring, she crept out from behind the barrel and had to climb carefully over their sleeping hulks reclining side by side on the floor, terrified of waking one. But God helped her make her way safely across. The old woman climbed with her out of the cellar, opened the door, and together they hurried as fast as they could away from that den of thieves. The wind had blown away the scattered ashes, but the peas and lentils germinated and sprouted and showed them the way in the moonlight. They walked the whole night until they came to the mill. The girl told her father everything that had happened.

On the day on which the wedding was to take place the bridegroom appeared, but the miller made sure to invite all his relatives and acquaintances.

When they sat at the table, everyone was supposed to tell a story. The bride sat in silence and said nothing. So the bridegroom said to her, "Well, my dear, have you nothing to say? Tell us a story."

Whereupon she replied, "Let me tell you a dream I had. I went alone through the woods and came at last to a lonely house with not a soul in sight, but there was a bird in a cage hanging on the wall, and it sang out:

'Turn back, turn back, young bride,
A murderer lives inside.'

"And the bird sang it out yet again. It was only a dream, dear heart. I went from room to room and they were all empty, and it felt so eerie everywhere. Then, finally, I climbed down into the cellar. There sat an age-old woman shaking her head. So I asked her, 'Does my bridegroom live here?' And she replied, 'Oh, my poor child, you've landed in a den of thieves. Your bridegroom does live here, but he intends to cut you up, cook you, and eat you.' Dear heart, it's only a dream. But the old woman hid me behind a great big barrel, and no sooner was I hidden than the robbers returned, dragging a girl along with them. They gave her three kinds of wine to drink – white, red, and yellow – which made her heart burst. Dear heart, it's only a dream. Then they tore off her fine clothes, cut up her lovely body on a table, and sprinkled it with salt. Dear heart, it's only a dream. And one of the robbers saw a gold ring on her little finger, and since it was hard to slip off, he took a cleaver and hacked it off, but the force of the blow made the finger fly into the air, bound over the great big barrel, and land in my lap. And here is the ring finger."

With these words she raised it aloft and showed it to everyone there.

As she told the tale, the robber turned white as chalk, jumped up, and tried to escape, but the wedding guests grabbed hold of him and handed him over to the authorities. Then he and his whole band were judged and executed for their evil deeds.

RAPUNZEL

Once upon a time there were a man and a woman who had long wished in vain for a child. Finally the woman had reason to hope that God would fulfill their wish. The little rear window of their house looked out upon a beautiful garden in which the loveliest flowers and plants grew. It was ringed by a high wall and no one dared enter, as it belonged to a sorceress who had great powers and was feared by everyone. One day the woman stood at the window and looked down into the garden, where she spied a garden bed planted with the loveliest rapunzels, or lamb's lettuce. They looked so fresh and green that she felt a sudden longing, an intense craving to eat them. The craving grew greater every day, and since she knew that she could have none of them, she grew wan and pale and looked altogether miserable. So much so that her husband took fright: "What's the matter, my dear wife?"

"Oh," she said, "if I can't have any of that rapunzel in the garden behind our house, I'll surely die."

The man, who loved her dearly, thought to himself, Sooner than let my beloved wife die, I'd better go get her some rapunzel, whatever the price. So at twilight he climbed over the wall into the sorceress's garden, hastily ripped up a handful, and brought it to his wife. She promptly made a salad of it and gobbled it up with great delight. But she liked it so much that the next day she wanted to have three times as much. If she was to be satisfied, the man would once again have to climb into the garden. Come twilight he lowered himself into the garden, but once over the wall, as soon as his feet touched the ground he had an awful fright. The sorceress was standing right there before him.

"How dare you," she said with an angry look, "climb into my garden and like a thief make off with my rapunzels. You'll pay dearly for it."

"Please forgive me," he replied, "let mercy move your heart. I only did what I had to. My wife spotted your rapunzels from the window and felt such a powerful craving for them that she would have died if she couldn't eat some."

Her anger quelled, the sorceress said to him, "If things are as you say they are, I'll let you gather as much rapunzel as you like, but under one condition: You must give me the child your wife brings into the world. Things will go well for it, and I will care for it like a mother."

In his terror, the man agreed, and when the woman gave birth, the sorceress appeared, gave the child the name Rapunzel, and took her away.

Rapunzel was the loveliest child under the sun. When she turned twelve, the sorceress locked her in a tower deep in a forest, with neither stairs nor door to enter and only a little window to look out of. When the sorceress wanted to get in, she stood outside and called:

"Rapunzel, Rapunzel,
Let down your hair."

Rapunzel had lovely long hair, fine as golden threads. As soon as she heard the sorceress's voice, she undid her braids and wound them around a window knob. The hair fell down a good twenty arms' lengths, and the sorceress shimmied up.

A few years later, it so happened that a prince rode through the forest and passed in front of the tower. He heard someone singing, and the voice sounded so sweet that he reigned in his horse and listened. It was Rapunzel, who in her solitude bided her time by letting her sweet voice ring out. The prince wanted to climb up to her and searched for a door, but there was none to be found. He rode home, but the song had so touched his heart that he returned to the forest every day to listen. Once, as he was standing behind a tree, he saw a sorceress walk up to the tower and heard her call out:

"Rapunzel, Rapunzel,
Let down your hair."

Whereupon Rapunzel unraveled and lowered her braids, and the sorceress shimmied up to her.

"If that's the way up," he said to himself, "then I'll try my luck too." And the next day when it started to grow dark, he went up to the tower and called out:

"Rapunzel, Rapunzel,
Let down your hair."

No sooner had the braids fallen than the prince clambered up.

At first, upon seeing a man enter the window, since she had never set eyes on one before, she fell back in an awful fright, but the prince spoke to her in such a gentle way, and told her that his heart had been so touched by her song that he could not rest and felt driven to see her. Whereupon Rapunzel stopped being afraid, and when he asked her if she would take him as her husband, and she saw that he was young and handsome, she thought to herself, He'll love me more than that old Frau Gothel, and said yes, and lay her hand in his. She said, "I'll gladly go with you, but I don't know how to get down. So each time you come, bring me a silk halter. I'll weave myself a ladder, and when it's done I'll climb down and you can take me away on your horse."

So they agreed that every evening he would come to her, as the old crone

THE ROBBER BRIDEGROOM

There once was a miller who had a lovely daughter, and when she grew up he wanted to make sure that she was provided for and well-married. He thought, If a proper suitor comes and asks for her hand in marriage, I will give her to him. Not long after that there came a suitor who seemed to be very rich, and since the miller found nothing wrong with him, he promised to give him his daughter in marriage. But the girl did not really like him, the way a bride ought to like a bridegroom, and did not rightly trust him – whenever she looked at him or thought of him, she felt a sense of dread in her heart.

Once he said to her, "You are my bride-to-be and don't even come to visit me."

The girl replied, "I don't know where you live."

To which the bridegroom said, "My house is out in the deep, dark woods."

She searched for excuses and said she couldn't find the way.

The bridegroom said, "This next Sunday you must come to me. I've already invited all the guests, and so that you find the way through the woods, I will strew ashes."

When Sunday came and the girl made ready to set out, she felt so frightened, though she did not rightly know why, and so as to mark the way, she filled both her pockets with peas and lentils. Finding ashes strewn at the entrance to the woods, she followed the trail, but with every step she dropped a few peas to the right and to the left. She walked almost the entire day, until, deep in the woods where it was the darkest, she spotted a house and didn't like the look of it, for it seemed so sinister and eerie. She went in, but there was nobody home, and there was a deathly silence. All of a sudden she heard a voice:

"Turn back, turn back, young bride,
A murderer lives inside."

The girl looked up and down and saw that the voice came from a bird in a cage hanging from the wall. Again it sang out:

"Turn back, turn back, young bride,
A murderer lives inside."

Then the lovely bride went through the entire house, from one room to another, but all was still and there was not a soul in sight. Finally she went down into the cellar, where there sat an age-old woman shaking her head. "Can you not tell me," the girl asked, "if my bridegroom lives here?"

"Oh you poor child," replied the old woman, "why has fate brought you here? You've landed in a den of thieves. You think you're a bride soon to be wed, but you will be wedded to death. You see, they made me fill a great cauldron of water, and once they've got you in their clutches, they'll mercilessly hack you to pieces, cook you, and eat you, for man-eating cannibals live here. If I don't take pity on you and save you, you're surely done for."

Whereupon the old woman led the girl behind a great big barrel where she could not be seen. "Be still as a mouse," the woman said. "Don't stir, don't budge, or else you're done for. At night, when the robbers are asleep we'll slip away – I've been waiting a long time for the chance to escape." No sooner came by day. And the sorceress noticed nothing until Rapunzel once let slip: "Pray tell, Frau Gothel, how is it that you're much heavier to hoist up than the young prince, who gets up so swiftly."

"Oh you godless child," cried the sorceress, "what vile things must my ears endure! I thought to have shielded you from all worldly temptations, and look how you betrayed me!" In her fury she grabbed Rapunzel by her lovely hair, struck her with her left hand, and with her right reached for a pair of scissors and snip-snap, the braids were severed and lay there in the dust. And she was so merciless that she took Rapunzel to a remote hideaway where the poor girl had to live in misery and want.

But on the evening of the very same day on which she banished Rapunzel, she tied her severed braids tightly to the window knob, and when the prince came by and called:

"Rapunzel, Rapunzel,
Let down your hair,"

she let the hair down. Then when the prince climbed up, he did not find his beloved Rapunzel but the sorceress, who gave him a nasty look.

"So," she sneered, "you came to fetch your ladylove, but the pretty little bird has stopped singing – the cat came to get her and will also claw out your eyes. Rapunzel is lost to you, you'll never see her again."

The prince was so heartbroken, in his despair he leaped out of the tower, and though he managed to come away with his life, the thorns in which he fell poked out his eyes. Then he wandered blind through the woods, ate nothing but roots and berries, and did nothing but weep and whine at the loss of his beloved. In this way, he wandered for a year and finally arrived at the remote hideaway where Rapunzel lived in misery with the twins she bore him, a boy and a girl. He heard a voice singing, and it sounded so familiar that he approached. And as he drew near, Rapunzel recognized him and fell into his arms and wept. Two of her tears wet his eyes, and wonder of wonders, he could see again as before. He led her and the children back to his kingdom, where they were warmly received, and they lived for many years together in joy and contentment.

SLEEPING BEAUTY,
OR THORNY ROSE

There once was a king and a queen who every day repeated: "Oh, if only we had a child!" But they never had one. It came to pass as the queen once sat in her bath that a frog crawled out of the water onto dry land and spoke to her: "Your wish will come true. Before a year has gone by you will give birth to a daughter." It happened just as the frog said it would, and the queen bore a daughter who was so lovely that the king was beside himself with joy and threw a great party. He invited not only his relatives, friends, and acquaintances but also all the weird sisters, the sorceresses, so that they would be kind and well-disposed toward the child. There were thirteen in his kingdom, but because he only had twelve golden plates from which they might eat, one of them had to stay home. The festivity was celebrated with great pomp, and at the end, each of the wise women gave the child a wondrous gift: the one gave virtue, the other gave beauty, the third gave wealth, and each, in turn, gave everything there was to hope for in this world. But no sooner had the eleventh sorceress bestowed her gift than the thirteenth suddenly stormed in. She wanted to avenge the slight of not having been invited, and without greeting anyone or even looking them in the eye, she cried out in a loud voice, "In her fifteenth year the princess will prick her finger on a spinning needle and fall dead." And without uttering another word, she turned and left the hall. Everyone was speechless with horror, when the twelfth sorceress, who had not yet bestowed her gift, stepped forward, and because she could not cancel the evil pronouncement but only mollify its effect, she said, "The princess will not die, but only fall into a hundred-year-long sleep."

Determined to protect his child from all misfortune, the king ordained that every spinning wheel in his kingdom be burned. But the good wishes of the other weird sisters were fulfilled, for the child grew up to be so lovely, virtuous, kind, and understanding that everyone who set eyes on her immediately had to love her. It so happened that on the very day on which she turned fifteen, the king and queen were not home, and the girl was left alone in the castle. She wandered everywhere, entered every room and chamber, and finally came to an old tower. She climbed the narrow winding stairway and came to a little door. In the lock, she spied a rusty key, and when she turned it the door sprung open, and there before her sat an old woman at a spinning wheel assiduously spinning flax.

"Good day to you, old woman," said the princess. "What are you doing?"

"I'm spinning," the old woman replied with a nod.

"What is that thing so lustily leaping about?" asked the princess, who took the spindle and wanted to start spinning herself. But no sooner had she touched the spindle than the evil wish was fulfilled, and she pricked her finger.

At the very moment she felt the prick, she dropped down on a bed that happened to be standing there and fell into a deep sleep. The sleep spread all over the castle – the king and the queen, who just then came home, began to yawn and soon drifted off, as did all their courtiers. Sleep fell upon the horses in the stable, the hounds in the yard, the pigeons on the roof, the flies on the wall, yes, even the fire flickering in the oven went still and fell asleep, the roast stopped roasting, and the cook who was just about to pull the ear of the kitchen boy, on account of some mistake, let go and fell asleep. And the wind went still, and not a single leaf stirred on the trees outside.

All around the castle grew a hedge of thorns that got taller every year and finally covered the entire castle, and kept on growing until nothing more was visible, not even the flag on the rooftop. But the legend lived on of the lovely sleeping princess – Thorny Rose, that's what they called her – so that from time to time princes came and tried to hack their way through the hedge of thorns to get to the castle. But they never made it, for the thorns held strong like stubborn hands, so the youths got caught in the tangle and, unable to tear themselves free, died miserable deaths. After many years, another prince came riding through the land and heard an old man tell of the hedge of thorns, that there was a castle hidden behind it, in which a lovely princess named Thorny Rose already lay sleeping for a hundred years, and with her slept the king and queen and all their courtiers. He had also heard from his grandfather that many a prince had come and tried to hack their way through the hedge, but that they had all been trapped in the tangle and died sad deaths. The youth declared, "I'm not afraid. I want to go and see the lovely Thorny Rose." The kindly old man tried to dissuade him, but he would not listen to reason.

But the hundred years had elapsed, as foretold, and the day came on which Thorny Rose was to wake up. When the prince approached the hedge of thorns, it burst into bloom before him with big, beautiful roses that parted in his path and let him pass through unharmed, and the hedge closed behind him. In the castle courtyard the prince saw the horses and spotted hunting hounds all lying fast asleep, on the rooftop sleeping doves sat with their wings folded over their little heads. And when he entered the royal dwelling, he saw flies asleep on the wall, the cook slumbering in the kitchen with his hand raised as if he meant to swipe the kitchen boy, and the scullery maid sitting in front of a black chicken ready to be plucked. The prince walked on and everything was so silent you could hear yourself breathing. Finally he came to the tower and opened the door to the little room in which Thorny Rose slept. There she lay, and she was so lovely that he could not take his eyes off her. He bent down and gave her a kiss. As soon as his lips grazed hers, she opened her eyes, awakened, and regarded him with a smile. Then the two went hand in hand down the stairs, and the king and queen awakened, as did the entire court, everyone eyeing each other with great astonishment. And the horses in the yard stood up and shook themselves, the hunting hounds leapt up and wagged their tails, the doves on the rooftop poked their little heads out from under their wings, looked around, and flew out into the field, the flies on the walls crawled on, the fire flickered in the oven and cooked the dinner, a roast began to sizzle, the cook boxed the kitchen boy's ears and the boy cried out, and the scullery maid finished plucking the chicken. Whereupon the wedding of the prince and Thorny Rose was celebrated in pomp and splendor, and they lived happily together until the end of their days.

CINDERELLA

The wife of a rich man fell ill, and when she felt that her end was near she called her only child, a daughter, to her bed and said, "Dear child, stay pious and good. God will always stand by you, and I will peer down from heaven and look after you." Whereupon the woman closed her eyes and died. Every day the girl went to her mother's grave and wept, and she remained pious and good. When winter came, the snow draped a little white shroud over the grave, and come spring, when the sun pulled it off again, the man took another wife.

The new wife brought two daughters with her, both pale and lovely to look at but cruel and black-hearted. Things went badly for the poor orphaned child. "We can't let the foolish ninny sit around all day doing nothing in her room," they said. "If she wants to eat, let her earn it – to work with you!" They took away her lovely clothes and gave her an old gray smock and wooden shoes to wear. "Just look at the proud little princess, what a grand getup!" They taunted her, laughed, and led her to the kitchen. She had to do hard work from morning until night, rise before sunrise, go fetch water from the well, light the fire, cook and wash for them. On top of which her stepsisters did her any nasty turns that came to mind, poked fun at her, poured peas and lentils into the ashes and made her pick them out. And in the evening, when she was weary from working, they gave her no bed to sleep in but made her lie down beside the oven in the cinder and ash. And since she was always dusty and dirty, they called her "Cinderella."

One day the father prepared to go to the fair, so he asked his two stepdaughters what he might bring them.

"Pretty clothes," said the one.

"Pearls and diamonds," said the other.

"And you, Cinderella, what would you like?"

"Father," she said, "I'd like the first stalk that strikes your hat on your way home. Break it off and bring it to me."

For the two stepsisters he bought dresses, pearls, and diamonds, and on the way home, as he rode through a bush, a stalk of winterbloom grazed his coat and knocked his hat off. So he broke the stalk off and took it with him. When he got home he gave the stepsisters what they'd asked for, and he gave Cinderella the stalk of grain. She thanked him, then went to her mother's grave and planted the stalk beside it, and she cried so hard that the tears dripped down and watered it. The stalk took root and grew into a great tree. Three times a day Cinderella went to huddle beneath it, where she wept and prayed, and every time a little white bird flew by and landed on a branch, and every time the girl whispered a wish, the little bird let fall what she'd wished for.

Now it came to pass that the king announced a great festivity that was to last for three days, and to which all the lovely young girls in the land were invited so that his son might pick a bride. As soon as the two stepsisters received their invitations they got all giddy, called for Cinderella, and said, "Comb our hair, polish our shoes, and fasten our clasps – we're off to the king's castle to make a royal match." Cinderella did as she was told but wept in silence, for she too wanted to go along to the ball, and so she asked her stepmother's permission.

"You, Cinderella," she said, "dusty and dirty as you are, you want to go to the ball? You have no clothes or shoes, yet you want to dance?" But when the poor child kept pleading, she finally said, "Here's a bowl of lentils poured into the ash. If you can pick out every one in two hours time, you can go along."

So the girl slipped out the back door to the garden and called out:

"Dear little doves, little turtledoves, and all the birds in the sky,
Come and make my poor heart glad
And help me sift the good grains from the bad."

Then two little white doves flew in the kitchen window, and two turtledoves flew in after them, and soon all the birds in the sky came flapping and flying down and landed in the ash. And the little doves nodded with their little heads and started pecking: Peck, peck, peck, peck. And then the other birds got to it: Peck, peck, peck, peck. And they pecked out all the good grains and dropped them in the bowl. Hardly had an hour gone by than they were done with it and all flew away again. The girl was happy and brought the bowl to her stepmother, thinking now she could go to the ball.

But her stepmother said, "No, Cinderella, you have no fancy clothes and you don't know how to dance. Everyone will laugh at you."

When the girl cried bitter tears, the woman said, "If in one hour you can pick two bowls of lentils out of the ash, then you can go," thinking to herself, She'll never manage. And when the woman had poured the two bowls of lentils into the ash, the girl slipped out the back door into the garden and called:

"Dear little doves, little turtledoves, and all the birds in the sky,
Come and make my poor heart glad
And help me sift the good grains from the bad."

Then two little white doves flew in the kitchen window, and two turtledoves flew in after them, and soon all the birds in the sky came flapping and flying down and landed in the ash. And the little doves nodded with their little heads and started pecking: Peck, peck, peck, peck. And then the other birds got to it: Peck, peck, peck, peck. And they pecked out all the good grains and dropped them in the bowls. Hardly had half an hour gone by than they were done with it and all flew away again. The girl was happy and brought the bowl to her stepmother, thinking now she could go to the ball.

But the wicked woman said, "It's no use, you can't come along, since you have no fine clothes and don't know how to dance. We'd be ashamed of you." Whereupon she turned around and hurried off to the ball with her two proud daughters.

Left all alone, Cinderella went to her mother's grave, stood under the tree, and called:

"Dear little tree, quiver and quaver,
Be my lifesaver."

Then the birds threw down a gown of silver and gold and a pair of silk slippers embroidered with silver thread. She hastened to slip into the dress and rushed to the ball. But her stepsisters and stepmother did not recognize her and thought she must surely be a princess, so lovely did she look in her golden gown. They did not give a thought to Cinderella, convinced she was back home sifting the lentils from the ash. The prince approached her, took her by the hand, and danced with her. He did not want to dance with anyone else and so never let go of her hand, and when anyone else came over to ask her to dance, he said, "She's my dance partner."

They danced until evening, whereupon she got ready to go home. But the prince said, "Permit me to accompany you," for he wanted to see to what family the lovely girl belonged. But she slipped away and leapt into the dovecote.

The prince waited until her father came, and he told him that the strange girl had leapt into the dovecote. The old man thought, Could it be Cinderella? And he called for an ax and a pick to break the dovecote in two – but there was no one in it. And when they entered the house, Cinderella lay there in the cinders in her filthy clothes, and a dim little oil lamp burned in the chimney. Cinderella had jumped out the back of the dovecote and run to the tree, where she took off her lovely gown and lay it on the grave, and the birds carried it away again, and then she slipped into her gray smock and sat herself down in the cinders in the kitchen.

The next day, when the festivities started up again and her parents and her stepsisters went back to rejoin the party, Cinderella returned to the tree that grew beside her mother's grave and said:

"Dear little tree, quiver and quaver,

Be my lifesaver."

Then the bird dropped down an even more splendid gown than it had the day before. And when the girl appeared at the ball in this dress, everyone marveled at her beauty. The prince had been waiting impatiently for her, and promptly took her by the hand, and she only danced with him. When others came over to ask her to dance, he said, "She's my dance partner." When evening fell she made ready to leave, and the prince followed her, wanting to see what house she entered, but she gave him the slip and dashed into the garden behind her house. There grew a big, beautiful tree heavy with the ripest, most luscious-looking pears. She climbed up the branches as nimbly as a squirrel, and the prince couldn't find her. He waited until her father came and said to him, "The strange girl slipped away, and I think she climbed that pear tree." The father thought, Could it be Cinderella? He called for a hatchet and hacked down the tree, but there was no one hiding in it. As soon as she reached the kitchen, she lay herself back down in the cinders, as usual, for she'd managed

to jump off the back of the tree, brought her lovely gown back to the birds, and slipped into her gray smock.

On the third day of the festivities, once her parents and sisters were gone, Cinderella went to her mother's grave and said to the tree:

"Dear little tree, quiver and quaver,

Be my lifesaver."

Whereupon the birds tossed down a gown more glamorous and glittering than any garment anyone had ever worn and slippers woven of gold. And when she arrived at the ball draped in this gown she looked so lovely everyone was speechless. The prince danced only with her, and when someone asked to take a spin, he said, "She's my dance partner."

Come evening, Cinderella prepared to leave, and the prince wanted to accompany her home, but she slipped away so swiftly he could not follow. But this time the prince was sly and had the stairway coated with pitch, so as she scampered down, the girl's left slipper stayed stuck to it. The prince held on to it – it was small and dainty and woven all of gold. The next day he went to the man, Cinderella's father, and said to him, "No one else will be my bride but she whose foot fits in this slipper."

The stepsisters were overjoyed, for they had lovely feet. The eldest took the shoe into her room to try it on with her mother standing by. But she could not fit in her big toe, the shoe was just too small. So her mother handed her a knife. "Hack off your toes – once you're queen, you'll never have to go anywhere on foot again."

The girl cut off her toes, swallowed the pain, and went out to greet the prince. Whereupon he lifted her onto his horse and rode off with her as his bride. But they had to ride past the grave, where two doves sat on the treetop and called out:

"Coo, caroo, coo,

There's blood in the shoe:
The shoe is too tight,
The bride is not right."

Whereupon the prince looked at her foot and saw blood spurting out. He turned his horse around, brought the false bride back home, said she was a fraud and that the other sister should try on the shoe.

Then her sister took the shoe to her room to try to squeeze her toes in, but her heel stuck out. Her mother handed her a knife and said, "Hack off a piece of your heel – once you're queen, you'll nevermore have to go anywhere on foot."

So the second sister cut off a piece of her heel, forced her foot into the shoe, swallowed her pain, and went out to see the prince. And he took her as his bride and rode off with her. As they went riding by the tree, two doves called out:

"Coo, caroo, coo,
There's blood in the shoe:
The shoe is too tight,
The bride is not right."

The prince looked down at her foot and saw blood spurting out, and that her white stockings were stained red. He turned his horse around and brought the false bride back. "She's not the right one either," he said. "Don't you have another daughter?"

"No," said the man, "except for Cinderella, a filthy little ragamuffin, born of my dead wife – but she couldn't possibly be your bride."

The prince said to send her out. But the stepmother replied, "Oh no, she's much too filthy. Such a creature dare not be seen."

But the prince insisted, and Cinderella was called in. First she washed her hands and face, then she came forth and bowed before the prince, who held out the golden slipper. Whereupon she sat down on a stool, pulled her left foot out of her heavy wooden clog, and slipped it into the slipper, which fit like it had been made to measure. And when she stood up and the prince looked her in the face, he immediately recognized the lovely girl who had danced with him and cried out, "This is my true bride!"

The stepmother and the two stepsisters were horrified and turned green with envy. But the prince took Cinderella on his horse and rode off with her. When they passed the tree beside her mother's grave, the two white doves called out:

"Coo, caroo, coo,
No blood in the shoe:
The shoe is not too small,
She's your true bride you met at the ball."

And once they'd finished cooing, they flew down and sat themselves on Cinderella's shoulders, one on her right, the other on her left, and there they stayed perched.

When the wedding was to be celebrated, the two false sisters hoped to curry favor with Cinderella and share her happiness. But when the bride and groom entered the church, the eldest sister to Cinderella's right, the youngest to her left, the doves flew down and pecked their eyes out. And so they were punished for their baseness and deceit and were blind until their dying days.

SNOW WHITE

O*nce in the dead of winter*, when the snowflakes fell like feathers from the sky, a queen sat sewing at her window, framed in black ebony. And as she sewed and happened to glance up at the snow, she pricked her finger with the sewing needle and three drops of blood stained the snow on the window ledge. And because the red looked so lovely against the white snow, she thought to herself, If only I had a child as white as snow, as red as blood, and as black as the wood of my window frame. Not long after that she did indeed give birth to a daughter with skin as white as snow, lips as red as blood, and hair as black as ebony, and so she called her Snow White. But no sooner was the child born than the queen died.

A year later the king took another wife. She was a lovely woman, but she was proudhearted and haughty, and could not bear anyone being more beautiful than herself. She had a wondrous mirror, and when she approached and admired herself in the reflection, she said,

"Little mirror, little mirror, hanging on my wall,
Tell me, won't you, who in the land is the loveliest of all?"

To which the mirror promptly replied,

"Your majesty, you are the loveliest in the land."

The queen was happy to hear it, since she knew that the mirror spoke the truth.

But Snow White grew lovelier day by day, and when she turned seven she was lovelier than the dawn and lovelier even than the queen.

And when, as she was wont, the queen once again inquired of her mirror,

"Little mirror, little mirror, hanging on my wall,

Tell me, won't you, who in the land is the loveliest of all?"

The mirror replied,

"Your majesty, you are the loveliest here, it's true,

But Snow White is a thousand times lovelier than you."

Whereupon the queen turned yellow and green with envy. From then on her heart sank to her stomach whenever she set eyes on Snow White – she hated the girl. Envy and haughtiness grew like weeds in the garden of her heart, for day and night she could think of nothing else. So she called for a hunter and said to him, "Take that child to the deepest wood. I don't want to see her again. You must kill her and bring me back her lungs and liver as proof."

The hunter did as he was told and led the girl into the deepest wood, and as he drew his hunting knife to pierce her innocent heart, Snow White started crying and said, "Dear hunter, let me live. I'll run into the heart of the forest and never come out again."

And as the girl was so lovely, the hunter took pity and said, "Run then, you poor child!" The wild animals will soon tear you to shreds, he thought, but still, it was as if a stone fell from his heart, because he did not have to kill her. And when a baby boar came leaping by, he killed it, cut out its lungs and liver, and brought these as proof to the queen. She bid the cook salt and sauté

them, and the evil wench devoured them, believing they were the lungs and liver of Snow White.

Now the poor child found herself all alone in the deep dark woods, and seeing all the leaves trembling on the trees, felt so afraid that she didn't know what to do. So she started running and ran over the sharp pointed stones and through the thorns, and wild animals leapt past her, but they did her no harm. She kept on running as long as her feet held out, until it grew dark, and there before her she saw a little house and went inside to rest.

In this little house everything was small, but so dainty and tidy she could not believe her eyes. There was a little table bedecked with a white tablecloth and seven little plates, each plate with its own little spoon, as well as seven little knives and forks and goblets. Against the wall, seven little beds stood one beside another, all covered with snow-white bedspreads. Because she was so hungry and so thirsty, Snow White nibbled a little greens and a little bread from each plate and drank a drop of wine from every goblet, for she did not want to take everything from just one. Once she was done eating and drinking, since she was so tired, she lay herself down in a little bed, but none of them quite fit. One was too long, the other was too short, but finally she lay down in the seventh bed and it was just right, and there she lay, commended her soul to God, and fell asleep.

In the dark of night the residents of the little house returned. They were seven dwarfs who dug and hammered for ore in the mountains. They lit their seven little lanterns, and in the flickering light they saw that someone had been there, for things were not quite as they'd left them.

The first one asked, "Who sat in my little chair?"

The second asked, "Who ate from my little plate?"

The third: "Who nibbled at my bread?"

The fourth: "Who sampled my greens?"

The fifth: "Who poked with my little fork?"

The sixth: "Who cut with my little knife?"

And the seventh asked, "Who drank from my little goblet?"

Then the first one looked around, noticed a sag in his bedcover, and said, "Who lay in my little bed?"

The others came running and cried, "Someone lay in my bed too."

But when the seventh one looked over at his bed and spotted Snow White lying there fast asleep, he called to the others. They all came running over and cried out in amazement, fetched their seven little lanterns, and illuminated the sleeping child. "God in heaven! God in heaven!" they exclaimed. "That child is so lovely!" They were so struck by the sight of her that they didn't wake her but let her go right on sleeping. The seventh dwarf went from bed to bed, spending an hour sleeping under the covers of each of his comrades, and so the night elapsed.

The next morning Snow White awakened, and when she saw the seven dwarfs she took fright. But they were friendly and asked, "What is your name?"

"My name is Snow White," she replied.

"How did you come to our house?" the dwarfs inquired.

Whereupon she told them that her stepmother wanted to have her killed, but the hunter charged with the deed spared her life, and she ran all day until she finally found their little house.

The dwarfs said, "If you will keep house for us, cook, make our beds, wash, sew and darn our socks, and make sure everything is clean and tidy, you can stay with us and you will lack for nothing."

"Yes," said Snow White, "very gladly," and she stayed with them.

She kept their house in order. In the morning they went off to the mountains to search for ore and gold, and in the evening when they came back, their dinner had to be ready. But all day long the girl was alone and the kindhearted dwarfs warned her: "Beware of your stepmother, she will soon find out that you're here. Don't let anybody in."

But after eating what she thought was Snow White's lungs and liver, the queen thought of nothing else but that she was once again the loveliest in the land, and went to her mirror and said,

"Little mirror, little mirror, hanging on my wall,

Tell me, won't you, who in the land is the loveliest of all?"

To which the mirror replied,

"Your majesty, you are the loveliest here, it's true,

But Snow White who lives with the little men

Over yonder hill and glen

Is a thousand times lovelier than you."

Upon hearing the mirror's pronouncement, the queen quaked and quivered with rage. "Snow White must die," she cried, "even if it costs me my own life."

She then retired to a hidden chamber to which no one else had access, and there she prepared the potion for a poison apple. It looked lovely and luscious, firm and white inside and bright red on the outside, so that everyone who saw it longed to take a bite, but whoever swallowed a tiny piece was doomed to die. When the apple was ready, she made up her face, dressed as a peasant woman, and set out across the seven mountains to the home of the seven dwarfs.

She knocked at the door, and Snow White looked out the window and said, "I dare not let anyone in, the seven dwarfs have forbidden it."

"As you like," replied the peasant woman, "but I'm tired of carrying my apples around. I'll gladly give you one."

"No," said Snow White, "I cannot accept it."

"Are you afraid of poison?" the old woman said. "Look here, I'll cut the apple in two. You eat the red part, I'll eat the white." But the apple was so artfully prepared that only the red part was poisoned. Snow White longed for a bite of the beautiful apple, and when she saw the peasant woman eat of it she couldn't resist any longer, stuck her hand out, and took the poisoned half. No sooner did she take a bite than she fell down dead. Whereupon the queen regarded her with horrid grimaces, laughed out loud, and said, "As white as snow, as red as blood, as black as ebony! This time the dwarfs can wake you."

And when she got home and asked her mirror,

"Little mirror, little mirror, hanging on my wall,

Tell me, won't you, who in the land is the loveliest of all?"

The mirror finally replied,

"Your majesty, you are the loveliest in the land."

Then at last her jealous heart rested easy, as easy as a jealous heart can rest.

That evening when the dwarfs got home they found Snow White lying on the ground, no breath blew from her mouth, and she was dead. They picked her up in their arms, looked in her mouth to see if they could find anything poisonous, undid her dress, combed her hair, and washed her with water and wine, but nothing helped. The dear child was dead and stayed dead. They lay her on a funerary bier and all seven sat around her and wept and wept for three days. Then they wanted to bury her, but she looked so fresh, just like a living person, and still had such lovely red cheeks.

So they said, "We cannot bury such loveliness in the black earth." And they fashioned a glass casket you could see through from all sides, lay her in it, and inscribed her name in golden letters, and that she was a princess. Then they set the glass casket out on the mountain, and one of them always kept watch. And the wild animals came and wept for Snow White – first an owl, then a raven, and finally a dove.

Snow White lay a long, long time in her casket and did not decay but rather looked like she was sleeping, for she was still as white as snow, with lips as red as blood and hair as black as ebony. It so happened that a prince went riding through the woods and arrived at the dwarfs' house where he hoped to spend the night. On the nearby mountaintop he saw the casket with lovely Snow White lying within and read the golden-lettered inscription. Then he said to the dwarfs, "Let me have the casket. I will give you whatever you wish for it."

But the dwarfs replied, "Not for all the gold in the world."

"Then please give it to me as a gift," said the prince, "for I cannot live without looking at Snow White. I will honor and adore her as my beloved."

Hearing these words, the good-hearted dwarfs felt pity on him and gave him the casket. The prince had his servants carry it off on their shoulders. It so happened that the servants stumbled on a shrub and the vibrations made the piece of poisoned apple that Snow White had bitten off fall from her throat. It wasn't long before she opened her eyes, lifted the casket lid, and sat up, alive again. "Dear God, where am I?" she cried.

Overjoyed, the prince replied, "You are with me." He told her what had happened and said, "I love you more than anything in this world. Come with me to my father's castle, and you will be my bride."

Snow White was favorably inclined and agreed to go with him, and their wedding was planned with great pomp and splendor.

But among the invited guests was her godless stepmother. Once she had decked herself out in all her finery she stood before the mirror and said,

"Little mirror, little mirror, hanging on my wall,
Tell me, won't you, who in the land is loveliest of all?"
The mirror replied,
"Your majesty, you are the loveliest here, it's true,
But the young queen is a thousand times lovelier than you."

In response to which the evil woman hissed a curse and was stricken with fear, so stricken she did not know what to do. At first she did not want to go to the wedding, but vain as she was, she simply had to go see the young queen.

And when she entered the hall, Snow White immediately recognized her, and the evil queen was riveted to the spot by fear and trembling. But a pair of iron slippers was already heating on the coals. They were fetched with a pair of tongs and set before the evil queen, who had to put on the red-hot shoes and dance until she fell dead.

LITTLE RED RIDING HOOD

There once was a sweet little girl. Everyone who set eyes on her immediately loved her. But her grandmother loved her the most of all. She showered the girl with gifts. One time she gave her a little hood made of red velvet, and because it suited her so well and she would wear nothing else, people took to calling her Little Red Riding Hood.

One day her mother said to her, "Come, Little Red Riding Hood, here is a piece of cake and a bottle of wine, take it to your grandmother. She is sick and weak, and it will make her feel better. Get ready before it's too hot out, and once you're on your way, watch where you're going and see that you keep to the path, or else you'll break the bottle and it won't do Grandmother a bit of good. And when you get to her place, don't forget to say, Good Morning, Grandma!, before you go poking your nose into every corner."

"I'll do everything you say," Little Red Riding Hood promised her mother with a handshake. But her grandmother lived deep in the woods, half an hour from the village. No sooner did Little Red Riding Hood enter the forest than she ran into the wolf. But she had no idea what kind of evil creature it was and was not afraid of it.

"Hello, how are you, Little Red Riding Hood?" said the wolf.

"Very well, thank you, Mr. Wolf."

"Where are you off to so early, Little Red Riding Hood?"

"To Grandmother's house."

"What do you have there under your apron?"

"Cake and wine – yesterday we baked, and I'm taking it to Grandmother, who's sick and weak, to make her feel better."

"Where does your grandmother live, Little Red Riding Hood?"

"Oh, about a quarter of an hour from here in the woods, under the three oak trees, in the house with walnut hedges out front. I'm sure you know the place," said Little Red Riding Hood.

The wolf thought to himself, The tender young thing, there's a juicy mouthful, she'll taste much better than the old biddy. Best be sly about it, and you'll get the two of them. So he went walking for a while next to the girl, then he said, "Look, Little Red Riding Hood, at the lovely flowers growing over there. Why don't you look around? It seems to me you don't even hear the little birds singing sweetly in the treetops. You're walking so stiffly, like you're headed for school, and you're missing all the fun in the woods."

Little Red Riding Hood opened her eyes wide, and when she saw how the rays of sunlight danced through the trees and how the forest bed was covered with lovely flowers, she thought, If I bring Grandmother a fresh-plucked bouquet of flowers it'll make her happy. It's so early, I've got plenty of time to get there. And she ran from the path into the woods to pluck flowers. And no sooner had she plucked one than she spotted a prettier one a little farther off and ran to fetch it, and so she wandered ever deeper into the woods.

But the wolf went straight to Grandmother's house and knocked at her door.

"Who's there?"

"It's Little Red Riding Hood, come to bring you cake and wine. Open the door."

"Just lift the latch, it isn't locked," cried Grandmother. "I'm too weak to get up."

The wolf lifted the latch, the door opened, and he entered without a word, went straight to Grandmother's bed, and gobbled her up. Then he put on her clothes, donned her bonnet, lay himself in her bed, and pulled the bed curtains.

But Little Red Riding Hood had run around fetching flowers, and once she'd picked so many she couldn't carry any more, she remembered her grandmother and set out again to her place. She was a bit surprised when she got there to find the door open, and when she went in, she had such a strange feeling that she thought, My goodness, I'm usually glad to visit, but today there's something wrong!

She called out, "Good morning, Grandma!," but there was no reply. Then she went over to the bed and pulled back the curtains – Grandmother lay there with her bonnet pulled down low over her eyes and looked so strange. "Oh, Grandmother, what big ears you have!"

"The better to hear you with."

"Oh, Grandmother, what big eyes you have!"

"The better to see you with."

"Oh, Grandmother, what big hands you have!"

"The better to hold you with."

"But, Grandmother, what an awfully big mouth you have!"

"The better to eat you."

No sooner did the wolf utter these words than he leapt up and devoured poor Little Red Riding Hood.

Once the wolf had satisfied his desire, he lay himself back down in bed, fell asleep, and started snoring loudly. A hunter just happened to be passing the house at that moment and thought, The old lady's snoring up a storm. Better go see if she's all right. So he stepped inside and as soon as he went over to the bed he saw the wolf lying in it. "Here you are, you old sinner," he said. "I've been looking for you a long time." He was about to empty his musket, but then he thought, the wolf might have eaten up the grandmother and maybe she can still be saved – so he did not shoot but rather took a pair of scissors and started cutting open the sleeping wolf's stomach. After a few snips he saw the red hood, and a few snips later the girl leapt out and cried, "Oh, how scared I was! It was so dark in the wolf's belly!" And then the old grandmother came out, still alive but hardly breathing. Little Red Riding Hood rushed to fetch a few big stones to stuff into the wolf's belly, and when he woke up he wanted to make a run for it, but the stones were so heavy that he keeled over and promptly dropped dead.

Whereupon all three were happy. The hunter skinned off the wolf's fur and went home with it, and the grandmother ate the cake and drank the wine that Little Red Riding Hood brought her and got better. Little Red Riding Hood thought, I'll never ever wander off the straight and narrow path again, if my mother forbids it.

It has also been told that another time, when Little Red Riding Hood again went to bring her old grandmother a piece of cake, another wolf spoke to her and tried to lure her off the path. But Little Red Riding Hood was on her guard and kept to the path and when she got to her grandmother's house, she told her that she'd met the wolf, that he'd wished her a good day, but he had such an evil look in his eyes: "If I hadn't been on the open road, he'd have devoured me for sure."

"Come," said the grandmother, "we want to lock the door, so that he can't get in."

Shortly thereafter the wolf knocked and cried, "Open up, Grandmother, I'm Little Red Riding Hood, and I brought you cake."

But they kept silent and did not open the door, so the sly gray creature crept several times around the house and finally jumped on the roof, where he planned to wait until sundown for Little Red Riding Hood to go home again. He intended to creep after her and devour her in the dark. But Grandmother realized what he had in mind. Just outside the house there was a big stone trough. So she said to the child, "Take this bucket, Little Red Riding Hood. Yesterday I cooked sausages in it, here – carry the water I cooked them in and dump it into the trough." Red Riding Hood kept carrying water until the big trough was full to the edge. The sausage smell rose up to the wolf's nose. He sniffed and peered down, and finally he stretched his neck so far out that he lost his balance and starting to slip. Then he fell from the roof directly into the great trough and drowned. Then Little Red Riding Hood went happily home again and nobody did her any harm.

SCHLARAFFENLAND

To Schlaraffenland I went, and there I saw Rome and the Lateran Basilica hanging by a silken thread and a man with no feet outrunning a swift horse and a razor-sharp sword that split a bridge. There I saw a young donkey with a silver nose chasing after two fleet-footed hares and a broad-limbed linden tree that bore hotcakes as fruit. There I saw a shriveled old she-goat carrying a hundred cartloads of lard and sixty cartloads of salt. Shall I pull your leg some more? There I saw a plow without horse or oxen plowing a field, a one-year-old child who flung four millstones from Regensburg to Trier and from Trier to Strasbourg, and a hawk swam across the Rhine and none would deny its right to do so. There I heard fishes making a racket that echoed all the way to heaven and sweet honey flowing like water from a deep valley in the cleft of a high mountain. All this, I tell you, was a sight for sore eyes. There were two crows mowing a lawn and two midges building a bridge and two pigeons tearing a wolf to shreds, two tiny tykes heaving two goat kids and two frogs threshing a bushel of grain. There I saw two mice anointing a bishop and two cats scratching out a bear's tongue. A snail came racing along and slew two wild lions. There stood a barber shaving off a woman's beard and two nursing infants telling their mother to keep still. There I saw two greyhounds dragging a mill out of the water and an old nag standing by, nodding her approval. And in the yard stood four steeds threshing grain with all their might, and two goats heating the oven, and then a red cow loaded loaves of bread into the oven. And there was a rooster crowing: "Cock-a-doodle-do, this tale is through, cock-a-doodle-do."

An Afterword
Facing Fears and Furies:
The Unexpurgated Brothers Grimm

A six-hundred-kilometer stretch from Hanau, the birthplace of the Grimm brothers, in the German state of Hessen, to Bremen, the destination of the fabled musicians, in the state of Bremen, has been designated as the Deutsche Märchenstrasse (German Fairy Tale Road). The road runs past Sababurg, supposed somniferous nook of Sleeping Beauty; the tower of Trendelburg, Rapunzel's alleged lockup; and Hameln, where the fabled Rat Catcher plied his trade. The Grimms have posthumously provided for a veritable industry, nearly as global in its distribution network as Coca-Cola. Countless selections of their tales keep pouring off the presses, nourishing imaginations in every language under the sun. But most delete the less savory details and leave out the darkest of the lot, candy-coating the content and tone. Disney's 1937 animated hit *Snow White and the Seven Dwarfs* set the modern standard of narrative nicety, turning the film's theme song, "Whistle While You Work," into an anthem to the Protestant work ethic, while judiciously deleting the evil queen's curious craving for the little girl's lungs and liver.

Why then issue yet another selection and translation of these tales? Because it is this translator-editor's hope to hereby salvage these enigmatic narratives from the insipid pabulum to which they have been reduced and restore the sting and the bite of the original.

For English-language readers, as for their German counterparts, the term *Märchen*, or fairy tale, is practically synonymous with the name Grimm, as though the genre itself spilled fully formed from the lips of the celebrated brethren, the pair attached in the popular consciousness like talkative Siamese twins. Inevitably, given the dark and cruel character of many of their tales, notwithstanding repeated attempts at expurgation – a process in which Brother Wilhelm himself already had a heavy hand – we likewise tend to conflate the name Grimm with its homonym *grim*, as in Grim Reaper. For the tales do indeed reveal monstrous intentions and recount cruel acts, like child abuse ("Cinderella"), child abandonment ("Hansel and Gretel"), mutilation ("The Girl with No Hands"), fratricide ("The Singing Bone"), incest ("All-Kind-of-Hide"), and cannibalism ("The Tale of the Juniper Tree"). They readily acknowledge fear ("The Fairy Tale About a Boy Who Set Out to Learn Fear"), greed ("The Golden Goose"), and desire ("Rapunzel"). They titillate like horror films and terrify like nightmares. But it is a playful – and therefore paradoxically comforting – terror, since as with scary movies and dark dreams, we know all along that it's only the stuff of fantasy and relish it all the more the *grimmer* it gets.

These tales captivate because, in imaginative terms, they tell it like it is, sublimating nothing, mining the tenuous realm of make-believe. Their enduring appeal, as Bruno Bettelheim reminds in his classic defense of the grim stuff in Grimm, *The Uses of Enchantment: The Meaning and Importance of Fairy Tales*, lies precisely in their bluntness:

> "Safe" stories mention neither death nor aging, the limits to our existence, nor the wish for eternal life. The fairy tale, by contrast, confronts the child squarely with the basic human predicaments.

Bettelheim then elaborates:

> The deep inner conflicts originating in our primitive drives and our violent emotions are all denied in much of modern children's literature, and so the child is not helped in coping with them . . . The fairy tale, by contrast, takes these existential anxieties and dilemmas very seriously and addresses itself directly to them: the need to be loved and the fear that one is thought worthless, the love of life, and the fear of death.

Let us acknowledge here and now, notwithstanding our best attempts to sugarcoat and coddle the reality, that childhood is a fearful state. Virtual victims dwarfed by powerful giants, children spend much of their time petrified of an infinite number of imagined and actual threats, and are themselves hardly innocent of violent intent. Biting, kicking, and scratching come before walking and talking. Even babes born with a silver spoon (or a stainless steel one, as the case may be) suffer and/or inflict oodles of actual or fantasized grief, and plow back the terror as imaginative mulch to mull over again at night. What children want in the stories they like and ask to be read or told again and again – what I remember wanting, and still crave now in the literature that matters – is a narrative drawn in broad elemental strokes, which acknowledges the mystery, the cruelty, and the terror, encompassing all the dark contradictions of life, and in so doing, defangs the threat, vaccinating the ever-vulnerable psyche with denatured venom.

·   ·

A word about the brothers and their background. Two of a family of nine children, six of whom survived, Jakob Ludwig Karl (1785–1863) and Wilhelm Karl (1786–1859) were born to Philipp Wilhelm Grimm, a privy councillor at court, and his wife, Dorothea (née Zimmer), the daughter of an apothecary, in a comfortable household in Hanau, in the principality of Hessen, at a time when Germany was a patchwork quilt of principalities loosely linked by a common tongue. Three occurrences – two domestic, one external – shattered the protected idyll of the brothers' childhood: the death of their father in 1796, and of their grandfather two years later, leading to the family's financial ruin; and in 1806, Napoleon Bonaparte's invasion and occupation of the Rhineland and the formation of the Confederation of the Rhine, an amalgamation of German city-states, electorates, kingdoms, and duchies under French dominion.

With a determination worthy of one of their fairy-tale protagonists, albeit with the aid of an affluent relative, Jakob and Wilhelm, both of bookish bent, studied law and gravitated to philology. Jakob worked for a time as a court librarian to the King of Westphalia, later joining his brother as a court librarian in Kassel. Both subsequently secured appointments – Jacob as a professor and librarian, Wilhelm as a professor – to the University of Göttingen, in the state of Hanover, where they lived under the same roof. Wilhelm married, while Jakob remained single. Both were dismissed, along with five other colleagues on the faculty, for protesting the revocation of the constitution by Hanover's autocratic King Ernst Augustus I, and were thereafter invited by King Friedrich

Wilhelm IV of Prussia to join the Academy of Sciences in Berlin, where they studied happily ever after. Their adjoining graves in the St. Matthäus Kirchhof Cemetery in Schöneberg, Berlin, are still a place of pilgrimage.

While engaged in various scholarly projects over the years – Jakob wrote extensively on the history and structure of Germanic languages, publishing a four-volume German grammar and later authoring a three-volume German mythology; together they worked on a German dictionary, reaching the letter F, and a two-volume book of German legends – the brothers are best known for their collection of *Kinder- und Hausmärchen* (Children's and Household Fairy Tales), a project they began as young students and continued to tinker with well into old age. Notwithstanding sluggish sales of the first and second editions, the work was reissued in seven large editions and ten small editions during the brothers' lifetimes, bringing them a modicum of celebrity, if not material comfort. But it was only in the late nineteenth and the twentieth century that the book, commonly known as *Grimms Märchen*, flooded the market in countless editions and came to achieve a popularity in Germany and abroad second only to the Bible.

Solicited by their friends, the writers Ludwig Achim von Arnim and Clemens Brentano, who compiled a German folk-song collection, *Des Knaben Wunderhorn* (The Boys' Magic Horn), Jakob and Wilhelm began gathering folk fairy tales for a planned sequel. The sequel never materialized, but the Grimms took the task to heart and ran with it. Culture and politics mingled in their motivation; sharing the burgeoning German nationalism of the moment stirred in response to the French occupation, the brothers found a scholarly outlet for their patriotic zeal. They set out to collect, and thereby preserve, what they believed to be an endangered store of popular German lore. As they put it in the foreword to the second edition:

This is how it seemed to us, when we saw that of all that blossomed in former times nothing survived – even the memory thereof was almost erased – nothing, that is, but a few folk songs, a handful of books, some legends, and these innocent household tales . . . It was perhaps high time to collect these fairy tales, for those who ought to safeguard them are fewer and fewer in number.

Or as Jakob would reflect, in retrospect, in 1841, they sought "in the history of German literature and language, consolation and refreshment . . . from the enemy's high spirits." By collecting and publishing these texts, they felt that they were "fostering national self-reflection." The first volume of what would become the first edition, published in 1812, was, in fact, intended strictly for scholars. It was only later that Wilhelm, the worldlier and somewhat savvier of the two, fathomed the work's appeal for a younger readership and modified its tone and content accordingly, elaborating on the spare folk descriptions and adding moral lessons to please and appease parents and educators. Still, scholars continued to take note. The second edition was line-edited by the philosopher Friedrich Schleiermacher.

From the start, the collection was, in fact, as much a work of fine-tuned fiction as of popular folklore. Pretending to tap peasant lore, the brothers enjoined friends to transcribe narratives from old books and sought their respondents among the neighboring gentry, notably in families of noble origin like the Haxthausens, who, in turn, sounded out their servants. And as for the purported Germanic folk purity of their sources, their favorite informant, the Märchenfrau Dorothea Viehmännin, a popular storyteller touted in the aforementioned foreword as "a peasant woman," was the wife of a tailor and herself of French Huguenot origin. The provenance of many of her tales proved to lead back across the Rhine to Perrault and other Gallic sources.

Nationalism was one of those nineteenth-century fictions whipped up in the frenzy of political self-affirmation, but geographic borders proved infinitely porous, and stories slipped between the cracks.

The Grimms have been accused of tampering with the narratives entrusted to them. Yet as Maria Tatar makes clear in her balanced accounting, *The Hard Facts of the Grimms' Fairy Tales*, "It is an error to see in the Grimms' collection printed transcriptions of oral folktales. The tales are simply too far removed from oral source material to deserve the title." Scholars have shown to what extent the brothers, and Wilhelm, in particular, raked through the material, deleting here, amending there, censoring, moralizing, and bowdlerizing. "But what name do they then merit?" Tatar asks.

> Clearly one cannot call them literary fairy tales, for, notwithstanding Wilhelm Grimm's unending editorial intervention, they are a far cry from the kind of narratives penned by E. T. A. Hoffmann, Hans Christian Andersen, or Oscar Wilde. The texts in the *Nursery and Household Tales* seem to lead an uneasy double life as folklore and literature.

The fact remains that their original source, that of a folk-narrative tradition passed on from generation to generation, still seeps through and speaks out, no matter how tinkered and tampered with the tales may be.

Their appeal spread rapidly. No doubt exaggerating a bit, the tall-tale teller Baron von Münchhausen declared that "In an old-fashioned German household, Grimms' fairy tales occupied a position approximately midway between the cookbook and the hymnal." And across the English Channel, in London, Karl Marx supplemented his little daughter Eleanor's spoken German with daily doses of Grimm. In an 1819 review in *The Quarterly Review* , an English journal, Francis Cohen, a.k.a. Sir Francis Palgrave, wrote appreciatively:

The most important addition to nursery literature has been effected in Germany, by the diligence of John and William Grimm, two antiquarian brethren of the highest reputation. Under the title *Kinder- und Hausmärchen* , they have published a collection of German popular stories, singular of its kind, both for extent and variety, and from which we have acquired much information.

The first English-language edition, titled *German Popular Stories* , edited and translated by Edgar Taylor, with illustrations by George Cruikshank, appeared in 1823 and proved an immediate smashing success. Three more English translations followed. Charles Dickens called Little Red Riding Hood "my first love," opining that "if I could have married [her] I should have known perfect bliss." Charles Dodgson (a.k.a. Lewis Carroll) hailed "the love-gift of a fairy-tale" in *Through the Looking Glass* . A generation later, in the midst of World War II, in his 1944 review of the Margaret Hunt translation, W. H. Auden wrote: "It is hardly too much to say that these tales rank next to the Bible in importance." He furthermore declared them "among the few indispensable common-property books upon which Western culture can be founded."

Meanwhile, back in the German fatherland, National Socialist theorists praised the Grimms' fairy tales as epitomes and models of the character of Nordic peoples, offering "a rare insight into the soul of peoples of German blood" and clues to the "primary principle of German character." It is true that the Grimms favored golden-haired princesses and heroes of solid peasant stock, and tapped popular anti-Semitic motifs that make the modern reader wince. In "The Jew in the Thorns," for instance (a tale not included in this selection), a Jew who tries to trick a fiddler is made to dance himself bloody among the thorn bushes as a prelude to his hanging, presumably to the giggling delight of little readers and listeners. But the questionable role of the Jew as villain in the German imagination was not invented or cultivated by the Grimm brothers, nor are racist tinges any more marked in their work than in that of other nineteenth-century *Dichter* and *Denker*, like Kleist and Nietzsche, both likewise posthumously conscripted to the Aryan cause. And while Nazi theorists had a field day interpreting the tales and extracting narrative elements in support of their theories, the scholarship was sometimes more questionable than the source. So a certain Georg Schott saw the protagonist of "The Brave Little Tailor" as "an altogether crafty character" in whom he divined definite Jewish traits. He furthermore viewed the giants in the same tale as "fine specimens of German manhood" who were taken in and victimized by the tailor's lies. "All this is truly Jewish," claimed Herr Dr. Schott. "We need only think of the brash publicity: 'Seven with one blow.' "

But according to the postwar German scholar Ruth B. Bottigheimer:

> It was not that the *Kinder- und Hausmärchen* themselves conspired to produce warlike behavior, but that decades of nationalistically steered propaganda had hallowed their "authors" as quintessentially German or Germanic, and therefore, as worthy standard-bearers for Germany at war. Wartime editions of the *Kinder- und Hausmärchen* poured off German presses.

For the British and American occupation forces in the immediate wake of World War II, the Grimms' fairy tales were considered taboo, practically akin to Hitler's *Mein Kampf*, and consequently removed from circulation in libraries and schools. But the German fondness for the fairy tale could not be expunged and the books were soon reissued, with some of the grimmer bits trimmed. Yet while it may not be too far-fetched to perceive an imaginative link between the oven of the cannibalistic witch in "Hansel and Gretel" and the human ovens of

Auschwitz and Treblinka, Nazi Party officials and functionaries and the German engineers who helped them realize their murderous schemes can well be credited for the mechanization and assembly-line efficiency of genocide, but the Grimms bear no blame for the blueprint. (Or does the right to bear arms, assured by the Second Amendment to the U.S. Constitution, reveal an innate violence in the American psyche that makes us more bellicose than others?) Any attempt to excise the cruelty of these tales, the very element that endears them to so many of their little readers, is to my mind as ill-advised and foolish as the ban on toy guns in a country where the real thing is readily available. For as W. H. Auden reminded: "No fairy tale ever claimed to be a description of the external world and no sane child ever believed that it was." To make believe is all about playfully working through the aggressive and violent tendencies innate to the human species, rather than unleashing them on one's playmates.

The sexuality in these tales is another prickly point of contention. Ever since Sigmund Freud's *The Interpretation of Dreams*, psychoanalytic theorists have kept busy finding phallic symbols, oedipal complexes, and penis envy hidden on every page. There is indeed an undeniable erotic subtext to many fairy tales, sometimes readily apparent, sometimes hidden at the metaphoric level. It is not too much of a stretch to recognize that Rapunzel's door-less tower represents her virginal body, to which her sorceress-chaperone permits no point of access for the prince. Nor need one necessarily be sex-obsessed to surmise a figurative allusion to something else in "Hans My Hedgehog" in the princess's fear of the prick of the protagonist's quills on their wedding night. And when the young protagonist in "The Blue Light" first steals the clothes of his invisible bride-to-be and later lays his head in her lap, surely I am not the only reader to respond with a libidinal rise.

The Grimms' tales have likewise been lambasted for their alleged sexism, to which the novelist Margaret Atwood offers a ready reply:

I'm always a little astonished when I hear *Grimms' Fairy Tales* denounced as sexist . . . It seems to me that traits were evenly spread. There were wicked wizards as well as wicked witches, stupid women as well as stupid men . . . When people say "sexist fairy tales," they probably mean the anthologies that concentrate on "The Sleeping Beauty," "Cinderella," and "Little Red Riding Hood" and leave out everything else. But in "my" version, there are a good many forgetful or imprisoned princes who have to be rescued by the clever, brave, and resourceful princess . . . And where else could I have gotten the idea, so early in life, that words can change you?

And as for accusations of these tales being wellsprings of authoritarian attitudes, there is far more revolutionary fervor and outright sympathy for the underdog here than any fondness for authority. In "The Master Thief," an ingenious burglar of peasant origin repeatedly hoodwinks and outwits a gullible lord and gets away with it. In "The Devil with the Three Golden Hairs," a good-luck child of humble birth tricks the treacherous and greedy king, who had intended to send him to his death, turning the tables on him and sending the king into eternal servitude as a doomed ferryman on the German tributary of the River Styx. Royalty almost inevitably gets the raw end in the Grimms' realm, whereas peasants and tailors claim the crown, turning social hierarchy on its head. The tasks the heroes of fairy tales set out to accomplish are humble takes on knightly quests, no search for the Holy Grail and the like, but hacking down and stacking a forest full of logs, fishing a pond dry of fish, and sorting lentils from ashes. But the humble nature of the task makes its accomplishment no less praiseworthy.

Some have perceived in fairy tales the residue of ancient myth. There is indeed a certain similarity between the trials of Hercules and all the impossible chores of fairy-tale protagonists, and a kindred motif in Danaë's father's attempt to keep his daughter childless in a bronze chamber open to the sky and Rapunzel's imprisonment in a tower with no point of entry. Might the marvelous minstrel in the tale of the same name, who charms wild beasts in the forest with his fiddle, be a distant relation or an heir to Orpheus? And when the servant Faithful Johannes in the tale of the same name is turned to stone on account of his loyalty and his master's folly, might one read into the prescribed remedy, that the king kill his sons, an echo of Jehovah's test of Abraham's faith on Mount Moriah?

Like Freud a century later, the Grimms were first elevated to near-saintly status and thereafter dragged through the mud, their tales accused of fostering every sin under the sun, before being sanitized and resurrected by Disney. These stories tap the unfiltered fundament of the collective unconscious as few others have before or since, dredging up ugliness along with beauty, bravery with cowardice, kindness with cunning. In uttering the unutterable, fairy tales retain the ring of truth. Which is why they have weathered the whimsies of successive social theories and political ideologies, and the passing fads and fashions of child-rearing, and why they are likely to stand the test of time for years to come.

As the Grimms' *Märchen* remind us, life is full of pitfalls and traps with ogres and witches at every turn. Nature keeps teaching seemingly self-evident truths to those inclined to listen. While the dragon of old may have gone extinct, global warming and drought are two intertwined modern monsters. Honeybees risk extinction if some simpleton doesn't come along soon to heed their warning. And a bloodthirsty virus is on the loose decimating the vulnerable. But there are hopeful signs. A handful of youths and maidens have been brave or foolhardy enough to take the jinni by the tail and topple seemingly omnipotent oligarchs in the land of *A Thousand and One Arabian Nights* , and others here at home have dared stand up to the hundred-headed fire-breathing dragon of multinational corporate greed. The rest of us children and addled adults, meanwhile, are forever getting bottled up in the infinite manifestations of our fears and furies. But instead of shying away, if we face them, as the long-suffering protagonists of "All-Kind-of-Hide" and "Hans My Hedgehog" do, redemption is sometimes a matter of shedding our old skin and discovering another. If there is wisdom in these seemingly simple tales, as I believe there is, it is in the promise of metamorphosis (frog to prince, straw to gold, hedgehog to human, tailor to king) and the potential force of metaphor to lift the spell of the mundane and point the way to a magical tomorrow.

Peter Wortsman

The Return of Little Red Riding Hood
in A Red Convertible
A Postscript

. . .

The girl goes driving in a red coupe sedan – no, make it a red convertible – to visit her dear old grandmother. The wolf tries to hitch a ride on the highway where you're not supposed to stop, and when he gets pushy she runs him right over. But the wolf, being resilient and conniving by nature, eats his way through the body of the car (a cheap import) and into the heart of Little Red Riding Hood. Now the wolf is squirming in the gut of the girl and she can't get him out and there is no emergency medical service for miles – nor would they know what to do if there were one, never having delivered a young girl of an invasive wolf. But the beast won't let her be. You'll learn to live with me, he says. Like hell I will! says the headstrong girl, who always carries a nail file in her purse and proceeds to cut him out, endangered species be damned. And scornful of speed limits, she makes it to Granny's with plenty of time to spare and whips up a tasty lunch of the leftovers. Granny gets indigestion and dies. Little Red inherits her pin cushion stuffed with precious stones and her automatic rocking chair, drives off distraught at breakneck speed into the sunset, and dies in a car crash. The convertible is junked, later to be recycled in the form of a thousand cans of Portuguese sardines pulled off the shelves following a few reported fatal cases of botulism.

Peter Wortsman

We gratefully acknowledge the following artists and institutions for the illustrations in this book:

Cover image, 10. 20x24 inches mixed media 2008, Pascale Monnin. Galerie Monnin 19 Rue Lamarre, Pétionville, Haïti.

ii	24x24 inches mixed media 2008, Pascale Monnin.
12	20x24 inches mixed media 2008, Pascale Monnin.
20	Fruits, Jean-Claude Legagneur.
30	Le chien de garde, Hector Hyppolite.
47	in *Galaxie Chaos-Babel*, Franketienne.
56	Fantastical Metamorphosis, Gesner Abelard.
59	Embarquement pour la Floride, Edouard Duval-Carrié. edouard-duval-carrie.com.
61	Pour cueillir la rose géante, Jean-Louis Sénatus.
67	24x24 inches mixed media 2006, Pascale Monnin.
73	in *Galaxie Chaos-Babel*, Franketienne.
85	Le lagon bleu, Phillipe Dodard.
97	Rétable des neuf esclaves, Edouard Duval-Carrié.
107	Baron, Edouard Duval-Carrié.
112	Recontre, ou Meeting, Franketienne.
137	Mariton, Marithou Dupoux.
145	30x30 acrylic on canvas, Pascale Monnin. Collection Toni Monnin.
162	10x10 etching 2003, Pascale Monnin.
176	Maître Grandbois, Lionel St. Eloi.
180	La départ , Edouard Duval-Carrié.
186	Prière du Pêcheur, Lyonel Laurenceau.
198	Fillettes, Jeanne Elie-Joseph.
201	Sans titre, Gregory Vorbe.
207	Femme au miroir, Jean-René Jérôme.
216	Jungle of Haiti, A.M. Maurice.

archipelago books

is a not-for-profit literary press devoted to
promoting cross-cultural exchange through innovative
classic and contemporary international literature
www.archipelagobooks.org